Heartland™
Winter Memories

Amy fetched the net, but as she started to go back into the stall she stopped abruptly and her heart dropped like a stone. Sundance was swinging his head around to nip at his stomach with his tail clamped close to his hindquarters.

It was one of the first things that horses did when they had colic.

"No, please, no," Amy whispered. Sundance swung his head around again, and Amy's heart jumped back to life and began to pound. Without waiting another second, she dropped the net and raced back down the aisle.

"Mom!" she shouted. "Mom, you have to come!"

Read all the books about Heartland:

Heartland™

Winter Memories

Lauren Brooke

To Lauren Grice, who loves Amy almost
as much as I do!

With special thanks to Elizabeth Faith

Scholastic Children's Books,
Euston House, 24 Eversholt Street,
London NW1 1DB, UK
a division of Scholastic Ltd

London ~ New York ~ Toronto ~ Sydney ~ Auckland
Mexico City ~ New Delhi ~ Hong Kong

First published in the UK by Scholastic Ltd, 2004
Series created by Working Partners Ltd

Copyright © Working Partners Ltd, 2004

Heartland is a trademark of Working Partners Ltd.

10 digit ISBN 0 439 95943 8
13 digit ISBN 978 0439 95943 8

Printed and bound in Great Britain by CPI Bookmarque, Croydon, CR0 4TD

6 8 10 9 7

Papers used by Scholastic Children's Books are made from
wood grown in sustainable forests.

Prologue

The day had been like so many others, but Amy was in high spirits, thinking of her family's plans for trimming the Christmas tree. As soon as she and Ty finished their chores, the festivities would begin. She was quickly making her way down the stable aisle, sweeping up hay and straw, but her progress came to a halt when the broom was ripped from her grasp.

"Sundance, what are you doing?" Amy exclaimed. She looked her pony in the eye and attempted to pull the broom handle from his mouth. "I need this," she explained. But the spirited pony bared his teeth, unwilling to relinquish his newfound toy.

"You rascal." With a firm yank, Amy reclaimed the broom and gave the buckskin gelding a playful look of disappointment. "Really, you should know better by now," she said, trying to sound angry. "You are no match for me in a tug-of-war."

The pony stretched his neck over his door and peeled back his top lip, as if he were laughing at her. Amy laughed and kissed Sundance on the nose.

"I'm glad *someone* is having fun. If you weren't so busy, I might ask you to help pick up the feed buckets!"

Amy looked over her shoulder to see her boyfriend, Ty, letting himself out of the adjoining stall. "Very funny," she retorted, tugging her jacket close against the cold December air.

Ty laughed and pulled back the bolt on Sundance's door. "Move over, boy," he said, after he had located Sundance's empty bucket in the far corner of the stall. The buckskin gelding laid his ears back and swung his hindquarters around. "Cut it out," Ty said as he stepped into the stall, but Sundance shifted again so that he had trapped Ty against the wall.

Ty placed his hand on the pony's rump and clicked at him. "C'mon, boy," he said with a trace of exasperation. "Can you tell your horse to move?" he called to Amy, who was watching with amusement over the door.

She shook her head. "Sorry. I'd like to, but I've got *so* much to do. I should get back to sweeping." She made her voice sound heavy with regret.

"OK, OK, you've got me . . . we're even." Ty pushed his dark hair away from his face and rolled his eyes.

"What's the magic word?" Amy asked sweetly.

"Now!" Ty raised his eyebrows. "Or you won't get your Christmas present."

"No need to be rash," Amy said, and then held out her hand to the pony. "Sunny, here boy," she coaxed.

The buckskin gelding swished his tail, flicking Ty in the stomach, and walked towards her. Amy slid her hand under his mane and rubbed her fingers in a circle. "Good boy," she told him as Ty retrieved the black bucket.

"He's far from good! He's the most stubborn pony Heartland's ever had," Ty grumbled, shooting the bolt home on the stall door. "I don't know how he's lasted here this long."

"Say what you like, but I wouldn't change a thing about him,"

Amy insisted. "Because then he wouldn't be my Sundance. We've been through a lot together," she added, running her fingers over the pony's velvety muzzle. Sundance had come to live at Heartland three years ago, when Amy's mom, Marion, had still been alive. Amy thought of how much had changed at Heartland since they had rescued him from that auction, malnourished and suspicious of everyone. Back then, she never would have dreamed that she and Ty would start dating. And she had never considered what life would be like without her mother's guidance and wisdom supporting her every step.

Ty touched her arm. "Are you OK? You seem miles away."

Amy shook herself out of her thoughts and smiled up at him. "Sorry, I'm fine. Come on, let's finish up so we can get inside and trim the tree."

"Sounds like a plan," Ty told her. "I'll race you."

Amy gave Sundance one more pat and finished sweeping while Ty gathered the last of the grain buckets.

"Ready?" Ty called at last with his hand on the light switch at the far end of the barn. Amy nodded and hurried down to the double doors where he was waiting. As soon as she stepped on to the yard, Ty clicked off the switch and pulled the door shut behind them.

The sky was totally clear, and the stars were a million pinpricks of white light shining on an empty indigo canvas. Amy tipped her head back and took a deep breath, drinking in the crisp winter air.

"Come on. I smell eggnog and cookies," said Ty, his breath forming clouds.

Amy slipped her arm through his as they walked towards the brightly lit farmhouse. "I guess you expect me to believe that you have an amazing sense of smell, but why do I suspect that you were in the kitchen earlier and saw Lou and Grandpa baking?" she teased.

Ty looked down at her and smiled. "I plead the fifth. Either way, it feels like the holidays are finally here," he said quietly.

Amy smiled back and squeezed his arm to show that she felt as excited as he did about their holiday. It would be nice to be home at Heartland for such a long stretch of time.

She climbed the stairs and pushed against the kitchen door, careful to avoid the prickly, waxy leaves of the holly wreath hanging on it, and immediately breathed in a strong aroma of cinnamon. "Something smells good!" she said appreciatively.

"No cookies for you until the boots are in the closet." Amy's sister, Lou, set a plate of star-shaped cookies on a tray that already held tall glasses of frothy eggnog. "You're just in time to help."

Ty and Amy slipped their boots off and put them away before following Lou into the living room.

"Wow! That's some tree," Ty said, staring at the bushy evergreen nearly eight feet tall in the far corner of the room.

"Isn't it a beauty?" Amy's grandpa, Jack, took the tray from Lou and placed it on the coffee table.

"I hate to be the bearer of bad news, but your beauty of a tree might have to lose some of its branches if I can't get it to stand up straight," a muffled voice complained from somewhere near the floor. Amy hadn't noticed her sister's boyfriend, Scott, crouching under the evergreen. "I've wrestled birthing cows with more luck!" he panted. "It seems totally lopsided."

Amy met Lou's eyes and grinned. While Scott was a talented and dedicated veterinarian, he wasn't terribly gifted when it came to domestic chores. Jack and Ty went to Scott's rescue, and the three of them managed to get the tree straight and to secure its trunk in the galvanized bucket.

"Turn it to the right. Now a little left," Lou advised.

"Perfect," Amy declared. The beautifully shaped tree almost touched the ceiling, filling the room with the sweet smell of pine.

"Now all we need are the decorations from upstairs," said Lou.

Scott straightened up with a dramatic groan. "Can you get those? We deserve a break!"

"Hey, I've been busy baking all afternoon," Lou retorted, heading towards the door. "That's typical. You work five minutes and need to sit down for an hour." She threw a sly smile in Scott's direction as she headed upstairs.

Laughing, Amy took the glass of eggnog that Ty was handing her and sipped at the warm, creamy liquid. She perched on the arm of the sofa while Jack, Ty and Scott sat down and dived into the cookies. Amy told them about Sundance's antics in the barn.

"That pony's a real character," her grandpa commented. "I've never known another like him."

"He's one in a million," Amy agreed.

"Thank goodness," Ty added, and quickly held his hands up in the air. "I'm only joking!"

Amy scowled at him, but she didn't mind Ty's teasing; she knew how much he cared about Sundance.

Scott glanced towards the stairs. "Lou's been gone a while. Do you think she's having trouble finding those decorations?"

"I'll go see what's taking so long," Amy said, getting up from the sofa. "Make sure you leave some of those cookies."

"Better hurry, then," Scott said with a grin, reaching for another.

Amy smiled back and made her way upstairs. She was glad Scott and Ty had agreed to help trim the tree. Having them there made the event feel even more celebratory. Her friends from school, Soraya and Matt, had promised to drop by later as well, which would add to the festivities. Amy was happy to be caught up in the spirit of the season. She loved any holiday during which she could spend all day with the horses, but Christmas always held an extra hint of magic.

She pushed open the door to her mother's room and saw Lou sitting cross-legged on the floor. A big cardboard box full of tinsel and red and gold balls was next to her, and she was holding an angel made out of gauze-covered cardboard folded in a cone shape, with yellow wool for hair. "I never knew that Mom kept this. I must have made it when I was about nine," Lou said.

Amy crouched down beside her. "Yeah, we always used it. Where did you find it?"

"It was in a tin at the back of her closet, behind all the other decorations." Lou turned the angel around. Scribbled on the back in childish handwriting was her name, *Louise Fleming*, almost obscured by gold and silver glitter.

"Look," Amy said, spotting a clear round container nestled in a pile of tinsel. She reached into the box and pulled it out. The container was filled with beautiful glass icicles, each one wrapped in a sleeve of tissue paper. "Do you remember these?"

Lou took the lid off and pulled out one of the icicles. She held it up and studied the light as it sparkled in the cut glass. "Of course. I bought them when I was still living in New York," she said. Her voice went husky. "It was Mom's last Christmas. I . . . I was only here for a few days, wasn't I?"

Amy nodded and felt her mouth tug into a smile.

Lou looked at her quizzically. "What?"

"It just seems so long ago. If only you knew the fuss Mom made before you arrived." She sat down on the floor beside Lou, hugging her knees. "I remember, I had these plans to go out with Soraya since it was the first night of our holidays, but Mom insisted that I stay home to clean up your bedroom." She shook her head. "I was so mad at her. It's weird to remember feeling that way."

"Yeah, I know," Lou said with a sigh. "There are things I would change, knowing what I do now. Still, I'm sorry my visit meant you had to stay home and clean."

"Oh, I guess I'll forgive you," Amy said with a laugh, glancing at her sister. "But I wouldn't have been so willing to forgive you back then. I just didn't understand you, and I guess part of me didn't want to..."

She gazed affectionately at her sister's golden head, bowed over the icicle. For the most part, Lou looked the same as she had that Christmas, yet Amy saw her in a completely different way. It was easy to forget everything that had happened since then, how much had changed for ever. For a moment, Amy closed her eyes and imagined that her mom was downstairs again, waiting for her to finish cleaning her sister's room.

Chapter One

"Unbelievable," Amy muttered, throwing a pile of horse magazines into a box. "She *finally* decides to visit and now everything has to revolve around her. She's not even getting here until next week."

Amy knew she was being overly dramatic, but she didn't care. It wasn't fair. She had had plans with Soraya for weeks, but now she was stuck at home with a can of polish and a duster.

Her sister, Lou, lived in New York City. She had a prestigious banking job, and hardly ever came to Virginia to visit. The last time she had stayed at Heartland had been in the spring. Now, she had suddenly called to say she was coming for Christmas, and, just as suddenly, Amy had to cancel her Friday night plans.

Amy kept grumbling, even though no one was around to hear. "I bet Lou's at some fancy wine bar right now having a great time while I'm stuck here cleaning her room." Amy had finalized arrangements more than a week ago with her best friends, Matt and Soraya. They all agreed the best way to celebrate the start of the holidays was a late night of movies, followed by pizza and ice cream. Amy had begged her mom to let her go. She had promised to clean on Saturday. But no, her mom insisted that it had to be done that very night.

Granted, the only reason her mom had asked her to clear out the room was because it was full of Amy's stuff, but that fact didn't improve Amy's foul mood. To her, it made perfect sense that her belongings should spill over into Lou's room, which was empty most of the year. Amy scooped up an armful of toiletries from the dressing table and cursed under her breath as half the plastic containers slipped out of her hands on to the floor. A lid came off one of the bottles and a cloud of talcum powder puffed up into the air before settling in a white ashy layer over the blue carpet.

"Great!" Amy muttered, dropping the remaining toiletries into a box. She heard a sound outside, and walked to the window. She pressed her forehead against the cool glass. *I could have been in line for popcorn now,* she thought in frustration.

She watched Ty, Heartland's sixteen-year-old stable hand, appear from behind the stable block. He crossed the yard towards his car, the full moon accentuating his high cheekbones and strong jawline. Amy sighed and ran her finger down the pane. For one crazy moment, she thought of opening the window, shinning down the drainpipe, and catching a lift into town with Ty. But she abandoned the thought almost immediately. She'd never do anything to get Ty into trouble with her mom. He'd only say no, anyway. Although Ty was always nice to Amy, he had complete respect for Amy's mom, who had been his boss for the last eighteen months.

Ty got into his car without noticing Amy watching from the window. She heard the faint rev of the engine and the car backed away from the house before disappearing down the long drive, the rear lights quickly fading from sight.

As she watched him, Amy began to sense that she wasn't

alone. She turned around and frowned. The room was still empty. Then a movement caught her eye. A pair of white riding breeches had been pushed through the partly open door. As she stared in surprise, they flapped up and down before the door was pushed further open.

"Truce?" called a voice. A pair of sparkling blue eyes appeared behind the jodhpurs. "Is it safe to come in?" Marion asked.

Amy shrugged and turned to look out the window again, but it was more to prevent her mom seeing her smile than because she was still mad. She didn't want Marion to think she was so quick to forgive such a grave injustice.

"I think my offer of truce has come just in time. It's like a war zone in here," Marion remarked, walking in and looking down at the powder-covered carpet. "A nicely scented war, though," she added, bending down and touching the spilled powder.

"Sorry," Amy muttered.

"No problem. I can vacuum it up later," Marion replied cheerfully. The mattress springs creaked as she sat down on the bed. "Are you thirsty?"

"Not really," Amy said, with another half-shrug.

"Well, I was thinking, if we took care of the rest of the room together, we'd have time to watch a video with a mug of hot chocolate. What do you say?"

Amy let her shoulders drop. It was impossible to keep up any pretence of being angry when her mom was obviously trying to make up for her missed evening out. She turned around again.

"Throw in some marshmallows and it's a deal."

"Done!" Marion beamed and patted the quilt for Amy to join her. "I'm sorry you had to cancel your plans with Soraya tonight," she said, and Amy nodded, accepting her apology but not quite able to say that she didn't mind. "I was just so excited by Lou's call that I wanted to start getting ready for her as soon as possible."

Marion reached across to pick up a silver picture frame from the bedside table and ran her finger over the photo of Amy and Lou as small children, playing on a seesaw. "You must have been three when this was taken," she said. "Which would have made Lou about eleven." She turned the photo around and propped it on her lap to show Amy. Amy knew it as well as any of the photos in the house. It had been taken the summer before their father's riding accident, which had left him temporarily paralysed. That accident had been the catalyst that had eventually divided the family. Her father had been unable to cope with his injuries and what they meant to his show-jumping career. He abandoned the family soon after he was released from the hospital. Just a few months later, Marion had left England to live with Amy's grandpa in Virginia. But Lou had been determined to stay in boarding school in England, convinced that their father would come back and they could all be together again. Though Lou's hope for a reunited family was not realized, she still didn't make much effort to visit her mom and sister in Virginia. Sometimes, Amy found it hard to remember that she even had a sister.

She glanced up to see Marion watching her. "I bet Lou's really looking forward to spending time with you," her mom said, as if she could tell what Amy was thinking.

Amy half smiled. "I'm not so sure about that," she confessed.

"It's never too late to start building relationships," Marion told her. "It's a shame that Lou can't stay to see the New Year in with us. Not that I'm complaining," she added quickly. "She's really busy with her work in the city, and she has lots of friends there, so she'll probably enjoy celebrating with them."

Amy reached up and plucked a strand of hay that was clinging to her mom's blue sweater. Marion could always find an upbeat way of looking at things, but Amy could tell by the strained lines around her eyes and mouth how much she missed her older daughter.

"You know, we'll have a lot to share with Lou," Marion went on. "There's the new training ring, for a start."

"You're right." Amy realized that it was just this summer that one of the pastures had been ploughed and filled with sand so it was appropriate for schooling. To save on costs, they had all pitched in to paint the perimeter fence. The end result was pretty impressive. Heartland would never have top-level facilities like Green Briar, the showjumping yard on the other side of town, but even Amy thought that the new additions made the place look really professional.

Amy had felt such pride the first time Marion had taken Pegasus into the ring and sent the beautiful grey gelding cantering freely around the perimeter. Since then, she had lost count of how many horses had been worked there.

"We painted the front barn in the summer, too," she

reminded her mom. Soraya and Matt had come over to help whitewash the stable doors as well as the farmhouse weatherboards, and Amy had been surprised by how much fun a painting party could be – though Marion had been less than impressed with the white footprints that had appeared on the kitchen floor.

"I think Lou will be amazed to see how much work we've done," Amy's mom agreed, putting the photograph back on the table. "Your sister has such an industrious nature. She has a real appreciation for hard work done well."

Privately, Amy doubted whether Lou would be that excited about all the improvements, but her mom's enthusiasm was contagious, and she began to feel her own mood change. It didn't matter that her older sister had been away so long; she was going to visit now – and for Christmas.

"You'll have to show her how well Sundance is doing," Marion added, getting off the bed to pick up a bottle of deodorant that had rolled under the dressing table. Amy felt her heart sink at the mention of Sundance, but her mom didn't notice as she took an empty cardboard box and began filling it with a pile of T-shirts. "He was still so sick when Lou was last here. I think he had his final bout with colic a couple of weeks after she left, didn't he?" Marion went on. "I bet she won't even recognize him now!"

Amy thought back to how neglected Sundance had been when they had first rescued him from the auction house. If her mom hadn't bought him, the pony might even have been sold for meat. He was gaunt, his coat loose and shaggy on his frail frame, but his spirit was fierce. His long battle with recurring colic had made him a picture of misery, but when his bouts of sickness had finally stopped, thanks to intensive care and supervised feeding at Heartland, his condition improved a hundred times over. Now he was a handsome part-quarterhorse with superb conformation. Marion had asked Amy to help get the gelding back into working shape, and they had been overwhelmed by how well he had responded right from the word go. He adored jumping as much as going on trail rides, and he tackled every fence with a spirit of determination and courage.

Despite his dazzling work in the schooling ring, Sundance had always been unpredictable. Amy remembered well that it had actually been his bad temper that had attracted her attention at the auction house. He had snapped and stamped at anyone who had come near him. No one had given him a second look. Still, Amy was drawn to him – she was certain there was more to the pony than a foul attitude.

Sundance's recent behaviour would suggest otherwise. Over the last few weeks, he had been exceptionally cranky, and it was Amy who had taken the brunt of his bad mood because she rode him most. She couldn't figure out why Sundance had started to act up. He had done so well for her at the end of the summer, but every time she tried to work him now, the buckskin gelding misbehaved. Just the day before, Sundance had pulled at the bit and then stopped short in front of fences. Amy knew Marion would be more than willing to help out, but she didn't want to add to her mom's workload. Not only did

Marion have her normal, demanding healing duties, she was trying hard to get all the short-term equine visitors back home for Christmas. And now that Lou was visiting, Marion would be even busier striving to complete Heartland work before the holiday. Amy crossed her fingers in her sweatshirt pocket that Sundance's bad attitude was just a passing phase that she could tackle on her own.

"I think Lou will prefer seeing Pegasus to Sundance," she said out loud, realizing she hadn't responded to her mom's mention of the difficult pony. "I mean, at least she remembers him." Amy knew that Lou had lost interest in horses after their father's departure, but Pegasus had been Tim's favourite showjumper, more like a member of the family than just another horse at their parents' successful showjumping stable. It had taken Marion a long time to nurse Pegasus back to health after the accident that ended his career as well as Tim's, but he was now fully healed and able to enjoy the trails as much as the other Heartland residents.

"Maybe we can persuade her to take a ride with us. She should be able to find the time since she's staying a week." Marion hadn't seemed to notice Amy's hesitation regarding Sundance. She picked up the box that was spilling over with T-shirts of every possible colour. "Can you open the door? I'll put these away while you finish up here. As soon as you're done, come down. I sent Dad out to rent a video, so who knows what he'll come back with. What do you bet he'll have *Gone With the Wind*? He seems to think it's the only movie I ever watch!"

Amy grinned as she slipped from the bed and opened the door for her mom. Whatever video her grandpa ended up getting, it would be great to spend some time together as a family, just the three of them. She quickly scooped up the remaining toiletries and clothes and dumped them in her own room before hurrying down the stairs.

Jack was just taking off his coat and scarf. On the coffee table in the living room were the two movies he'd selected from the video store. Amy bit back a grin as she picked up the top one and opened it. "*Gone With the Wind*," she announced as Marion walked in from the kitchen with a tray of mugs. "Good choice, Grandpa."

Marion shook her head and smiled as she put the tray down on the coffee table.

"It's your mom's favourite," Jack said, pushing the TV out from the corner of the room so they would be able to watch it comfortably from the sofa. He glanced up and saw the grin across Amy's face. "What did I say?"

"Dad! I must have seen that movie a hundred times!" Marion protested playfully.

"Well, they don't make them like they used to," Jack told her. "Besides, you always fall asleep if you're watching anything else." He clicked on the set and settled down in the middle of the sofa. He then looked at the tray in front of him and raised his eyebrows. "Hot chocolate and cookies? You're spoiling us, Marion."

"I just thought it would be nice to celebrate the start of Amy's Christmas vacation," said Marion, sitting down next to him.

"What she really means is that it was a bribe to get me to hurry up with Lou's room." Amy gave her mom a warm yet knowing smile and opened up the case of the second film. "*National Velvet*."

"Now don't you start complaining about that one, too." Jack held up his hands. "I had to drive all the way into town to get those."

"Us? Complain? Never!" Marion patted Jack's knee.

"No, really, Grandpa, *National Velvet* is great." Amy pushed the tape into the VCR and joined them on the sofa. Despite her earlier frustration, she couldn't help but feel content now. The best thing about any holiday from school was that she could spend more time with her family, and this one was even more special, with Christmas only a week away. "Happy holidays," she said, picking up her mug to clink it against Marion's and Jack's.

"Happy holidays," they echoed.

"To a wonderful time ahead, with the whole family together," Marion added, her eyes sparkling. "Just three more days, and Lou will be here, too."

Yes, thought Amy. *Three more days.* She crossed her fingers under the cushion on her lap, hoping that Lou's visit would turn out to be everything her mom was hoping for.

Chapter Two

Amy pulled a comb through her long, light brown hair and decided to put it in a French plait. It was great to have a leisurely start to the morning instead of having to rush off to school. She chose her favourite grey wool sweater, which matched her eyes, before heading down to the kitchen. She felt a little disappointed that her grandpa wasn't around. She knew Marion would be out in the yard already, but she'd hoped that Jack might be cooking some of his famous pancakes for the first breakfast of the holidays.

There was a warm, sweet smell in the room, and Amy smiled when she pulled a cloth off a plate on the table. Not pancakes – muffins! She poured a mug of steaming coffee and settled down to enjoy the freshly baked treats.

The clock in the corner of the kitchen chimed eight, and Amy realized that her mom had probably been up for a couple of hours without stopping for breakfast. She hurriedly popped the last few crumbs of the sugary topping into her mouth and put the remaining muffins on a tray along with two mugs of coffee.

"Morning!" Ty called when she went out into the yard. He had tied Pegasus to a ring in the wall outside the stable block and was smiling at Amy over the gelding's broad grey quarters as he swept the brush over the horse's winter coat.

"I thought you'd like some breakfast," she explained, showing him the tray.

"You must have read my mind! I was just thinking that it was about time you got out here to do some work. I mean, if it's holidays for you, we should get to take it easy, too," he said. The stable hand's face looked serious, but Amy could tell by the glint in his green eyes that he was just teasing her.

"Hey, give me a break. It's the first day of the holidays," she protested. "And it's not even nine o'clock." Amy caught herself as she said this, knowing Ty's truck often pulled into the Heartland drive well before seven o'clock.

"Holidays?" Ty walked around Pegasus and took the tray from Amy. The coffee was steaming thick curly threads in the cold, crisp air. "What're holidays? I've forgotten."

Amy laughed and stroked Pegasus's neck. Ty had started helping out at Heartland three years earlier. When he was sixteen, he had dropped out of high school to work there full-time. And it was true that he did work hard, often willingly stopping by on his day off to help Marion with the endless chores.

"Here, you can finish with Pegasus while I take this to your mom," Ty said.

Amy glanced down at her sweater. "I'm not really dressed for stable work."

Ty raised his eyebrows and gave a casual look around the yard. "Well, I guess we shouldn't have assumed that you'd want to be helping out on the first day of your holiday."

"Actually," Amy jumped in, "I had planned to get my history project out of the way. The sooner I can get all my homework done, the more time I'll have to spend out here, and to hang out with Soraya and Matt."

"That sounds like a good idea, but I think your mom was hoping you'd ride Hansel this morning," Ty said. Hansel was a stylish pony that was currently with them to be treated for behavioural problems, and Ty knew that Amy had developed a fondness for him during his stay.

Amy frowned as if she were struggling to choose between homework and riding. "Oh, all right," she said finally. "I guess I'll ride Hansel, then. I mean, just because it will help you all out. But it was a tough decision."

"OK, then I guess I'll take the coffee to your mom." Ty's laugh followed Amy as she made a hasty retreat to the house to get changed.

When Amy came back out to the stables, Ty and Pegasus were nowhere to be seen. All of the stall doors were open and a rivulet of soapy water was running down to the shallow open drain from the top stall. "Morning!" Amy called over the noise of the hose. She draped herself over the door frame and leaned into the stall so she could see her mother.

"Sleep well?" Marion asked, adjusting the hose so the jet of water hit a stain on the whitewashed wall.

"Yes, thanks." Amy stepped into the stall, over the stream of dirty water. She picked up the broom that was propped up in the corner and scrubbed at the dirty mark, avoiding the water that ricocheted from the wall.

Marion twisted the stopper at the end of the hose and let her voice drop back to normal as the water slowed to a trickle. "I'd

21

like you to ride Hansel this morning. Ty's out in the paddock setting up a course of jumps. I want to see how he handles the fences now that he's working nicely on the flat. He's more likely to bulge and pull if he's asked to do more intensive work."

"OK," said Amy, anticipating the challenge. "Do you want me to help you finish up here first?"

"I won't be long. If you can tack Hansel up, I'll meet you in the schooling ring. Oh, and thanks for the coffee and muffins. They were a welcome surprise!" Marion grinned, then wiped her arm across her forehead and turned the hose on again.

"You're going to wish I were around every morning," Amy joked as she headed around the stable block to the barn. The double doors were wide open and a cloud of dust particles that danced in the pale sunlight caught Amy's eye. Jack was carrying down a bale of hay from the loft. "Morning, Grandpa. The muffins were delicious, " Amy called as he walked past.

"Glad you enjoyed them." He sounded rather breathless as he headed towards the feed room.

Amy made her way up the centre aisle. Two heads appeared at the sound of her footsteps. A small bay pony stuck his muzzle over his door at the same time that Sundance's golden head looked out from the opposite stall. All of the other horses had been turned out in the paddock to make the most of the rare burst of December sunshine, but Hansel was staying in to be ridden. Sundance, on the other hand, couldn't be turned out while there was any chance of frost on the grass, because frost could bring back his old enemy, colic. The pony's system was still sensitive even though he had returned to full riding form.

Sundance's ears were pricked forward, and he tossed his head up and down as Amy approached.

"Hello, boy." She reached out her hand to rub his forehead. Taking her by surprise, Sundance swung his head sideways and sharply nipped Amy's arm.

"Hey!" She took a shocked step backward, rubbing the sore spot through her many layers of clothes. It was obvious that Sundance was still feeling bad-tempered, for whatever reason. Amy shrugged and turned away. There were other, less complicated horses at Heartland that needed her attention.

"Hello, handsome," she said to Hansel, relieved to hear his friendly nicker of greeting as she pulled back his door. He nodded his head, making his thick black mane bounce, and Amy smiled. Hansel's eager welcome was a sharp contrast to Sundance's cold reception! The bay gelding watched with interest as she reached up for the saddle, which had been set out on the high partition wall, then stood still while she tacked him up. He had impeccable manners in the stable – it was only when he was being ridden that the problems started.

Amy tightened Hansel's girth, feeling his warm breath on her hair as he swung his head down to see what she was doing. When she reached for the bridle the pony obediently opened his mouth to accept the bit. "Good boy," Amy praised as he chewed on the metal. She pulled his black forelock out from underneath the brow band and then clicked for him to follow her out of the stall.

Sundance kicked his door as they walked past, clearly bored

with being left in his stall. Amy sympathized with him. He couldn't possibly understand that he had to be left inside because they couldn't risk the frosty grass triggering his colic. "I'll take you out later," she told the buckskin gelding, but she couldn't bring herself to feel enthusiastic at the thought.

Amy led Hansel out of the barn and down the track to the training ring where Ty and Marion were waiting.

"Warm him up first, Amy," Marion called, pulling the gate open wide enough for Amy to ride Hansel through. The bay gelding calmly walked on to the soft ground, which was a major breakthrough in itself. When he had first arrived, Hansel would become impossible the moment he sensed he was going to be schooled. He would plunge and spin around in tight circles in a desperate attempt to escape from the ring.

His attitude with his owners had become progressively worse over a period of several months. They had finally discovered that his actions were the result of being ridden in a saddle that pinched him. By that time, Hansel had developed a fear of being schooled. The owners tried a new saddle and several other techniques before calling Heartland. It had taken Marion the last couple of months working patiently with him to cure his temperamental tendencies, and by using Bach Flower Remedies, she had eventually been able to break down his fear. He was now a much more accepting pony, showing the same willingness in the ring that he exhibited in the stable.

Amy trotted Hansel along the long side of the arena and did figures of eight to work him on each rein before trying to jump him. Although Hansel wasn't perfectly relaxed, he still obeyed her directions, occasionally flicking his ear back to the sound of her voice. Amy moved confidently with his strides, letting her hands give gently with the rhythm of his head. It felt so natural – she couldn't remember a time when she hadn't been able to ride. Her earliest memories were of sitting bareback with Lou while they were led around on their parents' showjumpers. She recalled the feeling of grasping her big sister's shirt when she sat behind, or being safely nestled in front where she could clutch the horse's strawlike mane.

Even though Marion and Tim's showjumping careers had ended, the family's commitment to horses had not. Marion brought the ailing Pegasus to Heartland, which had been her father's cattle farm years earlier. She nursed Pegasus back to health after the accident, learning holistic remedies along the way. Since then, Marion had built up an awesome reputation as a healer of horses that had emotional as well as physical problems, using a mixture of conventional and alternative treatments. As far as Amy was concerned, the best part was that she got to ride nearly all the horses that came to Heartland, from top-level eventing horses to much loved trail-riding companions. Hansel fit nicely in the middle of the spectrum – a loyal pony that had flair enough to earn high honours at local jumping competitions.

"Good boy." She patted the bay pony's neck and halted him in the centre of the ring. When she asked him to back up, Hansel stiffened and swung his quarters out, anticipating the familiar pinching discomfort along his spine, but Amy was ready. She squeezed more firmly with her outside leg and then encouraged him forward a few paces before asking him to step back again. This time Hansel calmly took three steps back and snorted with a toss of his head, as if he knew he'd done well.

Amy patted him again and looked at the course of six fences that had been set up in the adjoining field. "Do you want me to try the jumps now, Mom?" she called.

"I want to join up with him before you do," Marion replied, slipping off the gate where she had been sitting alongside Ty. She quickly jogged to the centre of the ring.

Amy dismounted and helped her mom run Hansel's stirrups up their leathers.

"He went beautifully for you. Nice work," Marion told her.

Amy smoothed the bay pony's neck. "You'd swear he wasn't the same pony that came here two months ago." Hansel snuffled at her coat pocket for a treat. "You aren't done yet!" she laughed. She gave him a final pat before going to join Ty at the fence.

"I never get tired of seeing your mom do this," he said without taking his eyes off Marion.

Amy pulled herself up to the top rail alongside him. "It's amazing every time," she agreed. There was something incredible in watching her mom gain a horse's complete trust by using the process known as joining up. No whips were needed, no force, just working with a horse's nature instead of against it. Join-up allowed the horse to decide to be with the person at the centre of the ring. It was a very powerful technique, and it was rooted in understanding the instincts of horses.

Hansel was already cantering freely around the arena, his

hooves thudding over the sand and sending fine particles up behind him in a cloud. Marion stayed in the middle. Each time she took a step forward, he slowed down. When she stepped back, the gelding lengthened his stride again, responding to his inherent sense that she was chasing him on.

Before long Hansel lowered his head and began opening and closing his mouth in a chewing action. Amy knew this meant that he was ready to stop running from Marion and would join her in the centre of the ring instead. Amy watched, fascinated, as her mom turned sideways to the gelding, not chasing him away any more, and waited. Hansel slowed down almost at once and swung into the centre of the ring, his eyes fixed on Marion. Calmly, he walked up to her shoulder and halted only an inch away.

Amy exchanged a delighted glance with Ty as Marion turned around to rub the bay pony between the eyes.

"I think that's your cue," Ty told her.

Amy slipped off the fence. Marion was already leading Hansel over.

"He's all yours," she said, patting the gelding's neck. "As you know, joining up shows how much Hansel has put his faith in people." Marion's voice took a serious, tutorial tone. "He needed to have that barrier broken down before he could be fully healed. It means that he now trusts us not to hurt him. So keep that in mind and be easy on him. Take it slow if you need to."

Amy nodded. It wasn't just Hansel that trusted her mom — she did, too, and she was confident that the gelding would go willingly for her now. She pulled down Hansel's stirrups and swung herself into the saddle. "Walk on, that's a good boy."

Hansel's dark brown ears flickered back, and he stepped through the open gate into the adjoining field. Amy cantered him around the jumps twice before pointing Hansel at the first fence. His stride didn't falter as he popped neatly over the red-and-white bars. But the second jump took them directly past the entrance to the ring, and even though Amy sat deep and drove him forward, the pony lost his concentration. He refused the fence and pulled to the left to try to charge through the open gate. Amy kept her seat and collected him quickly, turning him in a circle before aiming him at the jump again.

"Good! Use your right rein and give him more left leg," Marion called.

This time, Hansel flew over the fence with no hesitation and went on to finish the rest of the course without rapping a single pole. Amy finished by riding around the jumps in a slow canter, passing close to the entrance of the paddock. Although she could feel Hansel leaning towards the gate, he cantered right past, and Amy was delighted when she finally halted him. She patted his shoulder and gave the thumbs-up to her mom, who looked just as pleased.

"I think it's almost time for this fellow to be heading home," Marion said when Amy rode over. "What do you think, Ty?"

"Definitely." Ty pushed his dark hair off his forehead. "I bet his owners will be surprised when they see how well he's going now. Especially since they couldn't really figure out what was wrong."

"He has a kind temperament underneath all his bluster, but he was in a lot of pain. He needed to rebuild his trust and get some rest. Those things take time. He's only wanted to please all along," Marion explained.

Hansel snorted and stamped his foot. "I'll take him to the barn and rub him down," said Amy. She headed out of the ring, and her mom's words echoed in her head as she pictured an entirely different pony that was waiting for her in the barn. Sundance didn't exactly have what could be described as an eager-to-please attitude. Was that the reason why he still hadn't put his trust in her?

Marion came into the barn as Amy was untacking Hansel. "You did very well on him today. You anticipated what his reactions were going to be and responded with strong but sympathetic commands. You looked like a natural."

Amy felt a warm glow spread over her cheeks. When it came to riding, praise from her mom was something to be proud of — something that couldn't be taken for granted. "He's a great pony," she said, laying the girth over the saddle. "I'm going to miss him when he goes home."

Marion nodded. "But he'll leave a space for another pony that needs our help. Anyway —" her voice sounded brisk — "I came to let you know that your entry form arrived in the mail today."

"Entry form?" Amy looked at her mom, puzzled.

"For the holiday show I told you about. It's the day after Christmas. You said you might enter Sundance for the Large Pony Hunter class," Marion reminded her, resting her forearms on Hansel's stall door.

Amy wracked her brains and vaguely remembered a conversation about the show, but it seemed like it was months ago — before Sundance had started giving her a hard time. In fact, he had been doing well enough for them to have been champions twice that summer, once for Children's Hunter and the other time for a Large Pony Hunter division.

"I sort of forgot about it," she confessed. She turned her back as she took the bridle off Hansel so that her mom wouldn't be able to see her face. Marion could always tell if there was something wrong, even when Amy tried to hide her feelings.

"Well, maybe you should get some practice in this afternoon," Marion suggested. "He'll need exercising anyway since we can't put him outside."

"OK," Amy said. She kept her voice light, but inside she felt a familiar sinking sensation. It wasn't just because she and Sundance had been out of sync lately that she'd let his training slide; she had so many distractions in her life, with school and friends and all the traditional trials of being a teenager. She'd have to put in a lot of work to get him up to competition standard by December 26. Amy glanced over to Sundance's stall, where he was snatching at his hay net. How could she tell her mom she doubted that the gelding would cooperate enough for them both to be ready for the show?

After lunch, Ty offered to tack Sundance up while Amy finished washing the dishes. When she was ready to go down to the barn, she wondered what kind of a mood the gelding was in, hoping that it had improved from that morning. Her hopes for a miraculous personality upgrade faded when she walked on to the yard and saw Sundance swishing his tail and pawing the ground. At the sound of Amy's footsteps, he swung his quarters around in a one-hundred-and-eighty-degree circle, with Ty fighting to hold him steady.

"Someone's feeling fresh!" Ty commented over his shoulder. "He's raring to go. Do you want to lunge him before you get on?"

Amy thought for a moment, tempted by the prospect of putting off riding the gelding for a little longer. Then she squared her shoulders and told herself to stop being a coward. She would give Sundance a good workout on the flat instead to get rid of his extra energy. "It's OK. Can you hold him for me to get on?" she asked as Sundance danced on the spot, his hooves ringing loudly against the concrete path.

Ty held Sundance's reins more tightly as Amy reached for the stirrup and swung up into the saddle. The gelding snorted and tried to bolt forward but Ty stopped him with a firm yank on the reins. "Steady, boy," he said, putting one hand on the pony's chest. "I'm going to lead you down. OK, Amy?"

Amy nodded, too busy concentrating on sinking her weight deep in the saddle and keeping her legs still to object. Still, she wasn't sure if Ty was patronizing her by insisting on getting Sundance safely to the schooling ring.

Sundance jogged along, swinging his quarters out and high-stepping all the way down the path. He felt completely bunched up, his muscles taut and his head held high. The moment Ty released his hold inside the gate, Amy expected the pony to try to shoot off, and she was surprised when all he did was prance on the spot.

She decided to trot him for a while. Although Sundance pulled at the bit to show that he would like to go faster, Amy was able to keep him at a controlled pace with the reins tight and her legs scarcely touching his flanks. Flecks of foam mottled the gelding's neck as Amy rode him through serpentines. He bucked when she asked him to canter in the corner, but Amy pushed him forward. "No!" she said sharply.

Sundance arched his neck even more, tucking his nose into his chest, but he didn't buck again, and Amy cantered him until she was convinced that he was tired. "I think I'll try him over the jumps now," she called to Ty. He stuck his thumb up and pulled back the gate for her to ride out of the ring and into the adjoining paddock, where the course from Hansel's earlier workout was still set up.

Amy nudged Sundance into a canter in the corner of the paddock and turned him towards the first fence. The moment the gelding approached the bars, he raised his head and began fighting her hands.

"No!" Amy told him, closing her legs against his sides.

Instead of going straight for the jump, Sundance turned his shoulder and crabbed sideways, tucking his hindquarters under him. Just when Amy thought it was impossible for them to take the fence, he straightened and launched himself into the air. The top pole went flying, and Amy lost her balance. Sundance snatched at the loose reins and took off at a wild gallop towards the next fence. Amy grabbed the reins back as he gave a huge, unseating jump over the poles. Her stomach somersaulted as she was pitched on to his shoulder. She wrapped her fingers in his mane to try to stay on.

"Whoa!" Ty pounded across the paddock and caught Sundance's reins with one hand, using the other to help push Amy back into the saddle. "Are you OK?"

Amy nodded, but she didn't feel OK. She felt winded and her hands were shaking. "I'm fine. Can you hold him for a second while I catch my breath?"

"I think you should call it a day." Ty's green eyes narrowed with concern. "You've given him a good workout. Let me handle him while you take a break. That must have been scary."

Amy was extremely tempted to give up and leave Sundance where he was, defiant and sweaty in the middle of the jumping paddock, but she knew her mom would never end a session on a negative note. "I have to get him to go over a jump well, even if it's only one," she said, taking back the reins.

Sundance stood still when Ty stepped away. His sides were heaving and he held his head low. But as soon as Amy gave her legs a squeeze, she felt him tense up again. His neck stiffened when she asked for a trot, and several times he broke into a canter. Amy's insides felt numb after the shock of nearly falling off, but she tried to keep her seat and legs firm. She kept bringing Sundance back to a trot as they circled the paddock, and once she felt that he was settled again, she pointed him at a jump. This time Sundance cleared the fence evenly, but on landing he gave three large bucks, flicking his back legs into the air like a rodeo pony. Amy stayed on, but when she rode him up to Ty, who was standing at the gate, she was relieved to hear him say, "I'll take him now. I'll walk him around to cool off before he goes back to the barn."

Amy slid out of the saddle and gave Sundance's shoulder a pat, but she had to step back quickly to avoid her foot being crushed when he stamped his foreleg impatiently. "Thanks, Ty. I'm going inside to get a drink," she said, unbuckling her riding helmet. "Do you want one?"

"I'm OK, thanks. Look, are you going to talk to your mom about how Sundance did today?" Ty frowned as he looked at the yellowish froth covering Sundance's neck and flanks.

"He'll be all right," Amy said flatly. She didn't want to start discussing Sundance's behaviour with Ty. "Don't worry."

Ty looked closely at her for a moment, then gave a tiny shrug. "Maybe next time you ride him you should make sure one of us is with you, just in case he acts up again."

"Sure," Amy said, relieved that he wasn't pushing the issue any further. Still, she wasn't sure she wanted to enlist others to help her through her issues with Sundance. She walked slowly up to the house, her legs feeling wobbly. Her spirits lifted as she remembered that Soraya had called earlier and left a message for her to phone back. She had mentioned something about a party. Amy picked up her pace, her worries about Sundance fading as she shrugged off her riding coat. She was already running through what she could wear when she went out with Soraya. A party sounded like just what she needed to take her mind off Sundance's sour mood!

Chapter Three

The following day, Marion asked Amy if she wanted to go to a local dressage stable with her. "I've been asked to take a look at a gelding they're having a few problems with," she explained.

Amy looked up from her schoolwork. She had settled down at the kitchen table right after lunch, anxious to get as much of her assignment out of the way as possible before Lou arrived. Plus she wanted to have plenty of time with Soraya to get ready for the party at Matt's house. It was going to be on the twenty-third, the night before Christmas Eve, and Amy couldn't wait. She ran through her day's schedule in her mind to figure out if she could spare the time to go with her mom. "When are you leaving?"

"In five minutes," Marion replied.

"I'll go get ready," Amy said, after hesitating for a moment. She had been intending to exercise Sundance that afternoon, but she figured she could do it when they got back.

Marion was waiting in the car when Amy reappeared.

"All set?" she asked as Amy jumped into the passenger seat. She released the hand brake and the car quickly picked up speed as they travelled down the long, tree-lined drive that led to the main road.

"Yup. What's wrong with this horse, exactly?"

"The owner, Mr O'Brien, isn't sure. He told me that Rising Star is a five-year-old that has been competing for the last year in medium-level classes and doing very well. But recently his performance has gone downhill, and he's lost some suppleness in the lateral movements."

"Has a vet checked him out?" Amy pulled a pack of gum out of her pocket and offered a piece to her mom.

"Mmm, thanks," said Marion, taking it. Her fingers fumbled with the paper as she tried to unwrap it without taking her hands off the wheel.

"Here," Amy laughed, taking it back, peeling off the paper and popping it into Marion's mouth.

"Thanks, dear," her mom said, before returning to Amy's question. "That's a fair thing to ask, but Mr O'Brien wants me to look at Rising Star before he calls a vet. He says there's nothing obviously wrong with the horse. He's not off his food and he does just fine when he's doing regular flat work. It's only in the more demanding dressage movements that the problems start. I've spoken with Scott, and he's happy for me to take a look first."

Amy felt a surge of pride for her mom and the way that even Scott Trewin, their local vet, trusted her to assess horses before he tried a more conventional approach. Scott was actually the older brother of Amy's friend Matt, so he was as much a friend as a business associate.

They were driving down the main street, and Amy smiled at the window display of a fancy dress shop that had mannequins dressed as Santa Claus and his elves. "That reminds me," she said out loud. "Is it OK if I go to a party at Matt's house on the twenty-third?"

Marion pulled up at a red light and drummed her fingers on the steering wheel. "I don't mind since it's not a school night, but what about Lou? Do you think it's a good idea to go out when she's visiting? She's only here for a week."

Amy tried to suppress her irritation. She could hardly be expected to be with her sister twenty-four seven. It wasn't like they'd hung out together a whole lot before she moved to New York – in fact, Amy could not remember a time when Lou had lived with them permanently. She was in England for school and college, and then she got her Manhattan banking job almost immediately after relocating to the United States.

"I guess you could ask Lou if she wanted to go, too," Marion mused, steering off Main Street and pulling on to a winding country lane.

"Well, OK," Amy agreed, a little surprised. She guessed it might be fun if Lou came along. Her sister was used to a busy social life in New York City, so she'd probably jump at .the chance to go to a holiday party.

"Not long now," Marion said.

Amy looked through the windshield at the bare trees lining the road. "Does Mr O'Brien keep his horse at home?"

"No, he's at a small boarding stable," Marion said. "It's not one I've ever been to before."

A sign nailed to a tree ahead showed a black horse-shaped silhouette above an arrow pointing down a narrow road. Marion slowly negotiated the twisting drive, which opened on to a gravelled parking lot. She backed the car into a space alongside a horse trailer, and Amy didn't even wait for the engine to putter off before opening the door. She always loved visiting other barns and getting to know new horses.

At the end of the parking lot, a path led to a long line of box stalls that overlooked two outdoor arenas. In the smaller arena, a girl who looked around the same age as Amy was trotting a pretty black pony in serpentines, watched by a heavyset man wearing a dark green waterproof jacket.

Marion caught up with Amy and pointed to a showy-looking chestnut that was being led out of one of the stalls. "I think that must be Rising Star." The middle-aged man leading the gelding looked across and waved.

"I'm James O'Brien. Thanks for coming," Mr O'Brien said when they reached him.

"You're welcome," Marion replied. "I'm Marion Fleming, and this is my daughter Amy." Mr O'Brien nodded and smiled at Amy, who found herself warming to the thin, serious-looking man. Rising Star reached out his head to sniff cautiously at Marion, and she bent down and blew gently into the gelding's nostrils.

"It's the way horses greet one another," Amy explained, as a puzzled expression passed over Mr O'Brien's face.

Marion reached up to rub the perfectly formed star on the gelding's forehead. "Would you like to show me his paces?" she suggested to Mr O'Brien, who responded with a brisk nod. For a long-limbed man, Mr O'Brien mounted Rising Star with ease, Amy thought as she watched him swing his leg over the saddle. Marion didn't take her eyes off Rising Star as he walked down to the arena. The gate was already open, and the moment the gelding hit the soft sand, he began to trot.

"He's already anxious," Marion murmured, closing the gate and resting her forearms on it. A sudden breeze blew her wavy blonde hair across her cheek, and she reached up to tuck it back behind her ear.

"He's clamping his tail down," Amy agreed. She knew that was a sure sign that a horse was discontented. If Rising Star had been enjoying his work, he would have been holding his tail higher, letting it flow out behind him like a chestnut banner.

Marion lapsed into silence as Mr O'Brien took Rising Star through his paces. The gelding responded obediently with his neck arched, and, other than his tail, there was no outward sign that he was unhappy.

At the top of the arena, Mr O'Brien turned to leg yield Rising Star diagonally across the ring. Amy immediately saw why he had called her mother to look at the horse. Even though Mr O'Brien still sat quietly, giving invisible commands with his hands and legs, Rising Star had completely lost his form. The smooth outline of his body had collapsed. His nose came up, hollowing his neck and spine, and his stride became short and choppy, nothing like the fluid, elegant moves that Amy would have expected from a top dressage horse. The horse was supposed to be crossing its legs as it angled across the centre of the ring, but the movement was stilted as the horse twisted away from his rider's light commands.

Marion opened the gate and waved to catch Mr O'Brien's attention. "I've seen enough, thanks," she called.

Mr O'Brien halted Rising Star and patted his damp shoulder. "Do you know what's wrong with him?"

"I'd like to look at him without his saddle before I say anything. Would you take him up to his stall and untack him, please?"

"What do you think it is, Mom?" Amy asked as they followed behind Rising Star.

"Did you have any ideas while you were watching him?"

Amy shook her head. "He really stiffened up when he was asked to move laterally, so I'd guess that something is hurting him. But I don't know what it could be. Maybe his saddle is pinching, like Hansel's?"

Marion smiled. "You're right to think about the tack. It's often the last thing that occurs to people, but they'd be quick enough to complain if their shoes were too tight, wouldn't they?" She gave Amy a lighthearted elbow. "It's the same for a horse, or worse, since they are carrying additional weight. That was an informed guess, Amy, but I don't think it's the case with Rising Star."

They arrived outside Rising Star's stall just as Mr O'Brien was placing the saddle over the half door. Amy waited while Marion let herself into the stall and placed her hands on either side of the gelding's withers. She began to apply pressure with the flats of her fingers, lightly at first and then more firmly, all the way down his spine. When she reached the centre of Rising Star's back, the gelding suddenly put his ears back.

Marion murmured soothingly and probed around the area with her fingers. "Come look at this," she invited Amy.

Amy stepped closer. As Marion's fingers pressed against the centre of the gelding's back once again, she could see him actually shrink away from her mother's touch.

"Feel right here. The area is a little harder than you'd expect," Marion told her.

Amy reached out her hand and gently pressed. "It feels hot, too," she remarked.

Marion flashed her a quick smile before looking up at Mr O'Brien, who was holding the gelding and watching them with a concerned expression. "I'm fairly sure that Rising Star has damaged his back," she said. "It isn't terribly serious. It could be from something as simple as catching himself on a stone when he was rolling in a field. Regardless, it hasn't had the chance to heal because of his ongoing work. Marion rubbed Rising Star's neck as she spoke. "The saddle could irritate it, but I think the dressage work is what is really hindering his recovery — especially since he's working on a deep sand surface, which can be hard on a horse's muscles. And lateral movements put the most strain on a horse's back, so that's why you notice the relatively minor injury then."

"That would make sense," Mr O'Brien agreed, looking even more subdued. "What do you suggest I do?"

"Well, you could start by giving Scott Trewin a call. He'll probably recommend a course of anti-inflammatory drugs to reduce the heat and swelling," Marion explained, patting Rising Star's neck.

Mr O'Brien blinked. "Can't you fix it?"

"I always work alongside conventional medicine," Marion

told him. "Especially when there are some excellent drugs available for injuries like this." She pulled a piece of paper and a pencil from her pocket and began making notes. "I'd also suggest you massage some arnica cream into his back. Lavender oil would be a good idea, too. The scent will relax Rising Star, but it also has anti-inflammatory properties."

"How do I use it?" Mr O'Brien asked.

Amy slipped out of the stable as her mom began to describe the healing properties of arnica and lavender in more detail. She knew that Marion often used them at Heartland, and Amy wasn't interested in listening to her mom explain all the details to Mr O'Brien. She decided to see if there was anyone riding in the other outdoor arena instead.

When she walked away from the stables she was surprised to see that the black pony was still being exercised. "They're giving her quite a workout," Amy murmured under her breath, making her way down to the perimeter fence to watch the pretty, dish-faced mare. With her romantically arched neck and delicate movements, it looked like she had some Arabian blood in her. As the pony passed Amy at a trot, she could hear her laboured breath.

"Come on, Jess, you're not using your legs properly! Squeeze!"

Amy glanced across to the gate where the heavyset man was watching. She guessed that the girl on the pony was his daughter.

"I am using my legs, Dad. Jasmine's just being stubborn," the girl yelled over her shoulder.

As they came down the centre line, Amy saw that the girl was trying to get the mare to do an extended trot. She was sitting deep in the saddle and closing her heels against the pony's flanks, but the mare was refusing to extend. She kept going faster instead, uncertain of what her rider wanted. Then Amy noticed that every time the mare's legs hit the sand, she seemed uncomfortable, flinching away from putting any weight on them.

"Oh, come on, give her a break," Amy muttered, flashing an angry glance at the man standing at the gate.

As if he had heard her, he waved his arms in the air. "I give up. Bring her in. If you can't get her to do what you want, we'll have to get rid of her."

Even from a distance, Amy could see that his cheeks were flushed with annoyance. She felt sorry for the mare as the girl turned her more sharply than necessary to walk through the gate.

"Unbelievable," she murmured, shaking her head with disgust.

"What is?"

Amy jumped at the voice behind her. "Hi, Mom. I didn't hear you." She waved her hand at the black mare being led up to the stable block and told her mom what had happened.

Marion's blue eyes darkened. "I hate it when people treat horses like machines. At least Mr O'Brien cares more about Rising Star than he does about his dressage career. From the sound of it, he's going to buy all the remedies I suggested right away! That's always the most satisfying kind of horse owner to work with."

Amy turned to walk to the car with her mom and thought back to Marion's own successful showjumping career, which she had given up to heal damaged horses instead. When her mom made comments about people treating horses like machines, she realized there was another, far less attractive side to competing.

"Shows aren't connected with the happiness of the horse at all," she agreed out loud. She hesitated as Marion slid the key into the car door. "You know, I really don't mind missing the show the day after Christmas, especially if it means Sundance will be spared some of that pressure."

Marion gave her daughter a long look across the roof of the car. "Just because there are some people who abuse the system, it doesn't mean that competitions are a bad idea in themselves. Most horses love competing. I was just saying that, as an owner, you have to look after a horse's welfare. That should always come before winning." She laughed and shook her head as she opened the car door. "You know, Sundance is a born competitor. So it's OK, you don't have to worry about entering him in the holiday show." She ducked into the car, leaning over to open the door for Amy. "He'll have a great time, and I know you will, too."

"Terrific," Amy said, getting in and reaching for her seat belt. "I can't wait."

Chapter Four

"Mmm, I love the taste of the cinnamon in this," Soraya remarked over the sound of Christmas songs from the jukebox in the corner of the café. She took another sip of her hot chocolate and let out an exaggerated sigh of contentment.

"You've got cream on your nose," Amy pointed out with a smile. Soraya had called her first thing that morning to invite her into town along with Matt so they could shop for their Christmas presents together. They had hit all the major stores, and Amy had managed to get nearly all of her gifts. She was feeling exhausted now – the mall was heaving with people, and every checkout counter had boasted a long line.

While Soraya picked up a napkin and dabbed at her nose, Amy's attention was distracted by Matt Trewin pulling out a chair next to her. "They make the best ice-cream sodas here," he said enthusiastically, putting down a tall glass filled to the brim with frothy liquid.

"Only you could enjoy an ice-based drink when it's like Siberia outside," Soraya told him.

"It's not that cold, Ms Martin. Honestly, you guys need to toughen up." He shook his head with mock pity. "It's not even below freezing."

"Hey, who are you talking to?" Amy playfully punched his arm. "If you want to be tough, come muck out ten horse stalls at six in the morning. It'll feel cold then," she said. The moment the words were out of her mouth she felt a guilty lurch in her stomach. She hadn't got up early once to help her mom since the Christmas break had begun.

"You'd better can it, Trewin. You're outnumbered two to one," Soraya pointed out.

"You're assuming that quantity is more important than quality," Matt argued, with a devious glint in his brown eyes.

"Time out!" Amy held up her hands. "'Tis the season to be jolly and all that."

"You're right, you're right. And as proof of my goodwill, I'll buy you both a cinnamon roll," Matt said, pushing out his chair and jingling the loose change in his pocket.

"Yeah, and mine will be laced with arsenic?" Soraya asked with a laugh.

"You guessed it." Matt winked at Soraya. "But since Amy's been on her best behaviour, she can have extra icing." He smiled at Amy before heading over to the bakery counter.

"He so likes you," Soraya said, dropping her voice to a stage whisper that Amy was sure everyone in that wing of the mall could hear, from the Baby Gap to the bookshop.

"Enough already! He's just a good friend," Amy insisted, but she could feel her cheeks beginning to burn and looked down at her half-empty mug of hot chocolate.

"Yeah, right, and he just happens to be buying you a cinnamon roll because he thinks you need the extra calories," Soraya retorted, her voice heavy with sarcasm.

"He's buying you one, too," Amy pointed out.

"Come on, Amy! He could hardly buy one for you and not for me, could he? I don't get why you keep denying the chemistry between you. Matt's totally cute."

"And so totally not right for me."

"What? Because he's not a professional showjumper? Is it always about horses with you?" Soraya interrogated, despite already knowing the answer. "So, have you ridden much this holiday?" she asked, flipping back her curly black hair and taking another sip of her hot chocolate. "Are you still going to that show?"

Amy stared at Soraya. "You heard about the show?"

"You mentioned it a while ago." Soraya was concentrating on licking the whipped cream off her straw. "Something about taking Sundance."

"Oh," Amy replied nonchalantly. "Well, I'm not so sure I'll have time to go now that Lou's coming." Amy stirred her spoon in her mug and watched the cream whirl around in a frothy spiral. By the time she had got back from the dressage stable yesterday, it had been almost dark, so she had decided to turn Sundance loose in the schooling ring for twenty minutes instead of riding him. He had refused to be caught after stretching his legs, and when she had cornered him, the buckskin gelding had tried to kick her. "I'm going to ride Sundance later today," she said vaguely.

Soraya was watching her closely. "What's wrong?"

Amy looked up. Soraya shared Amy's passion for riding and came to help out at Heartland on a regular basis. Even though her best friend teased her about being more obsessed with horses than with boys, Amy knew Soraya understood her dedication. It was no good bluffing; Soraya knew her too well. "I'm having a few problems with Sundance at the moment," she admitted.

"Like what?" Soraya leaned her arms on the table as Amy began to describe Sundance's bad behaviour over the last few weeks.

"Have you asked your mom to look at him?" Soraya asked.

"Not yet. I don't want to worry her. Anyway, there's nothing wrong with him – he's just plain moody." Amy felt a surge of resentment as she thought about the buckskin gelding's attitude.

"But he was doing so well for you in the summer," Soraya reminded her. "He looked great in those shows!"

"Absolutely. You'd think two champion ribbons would be enough for my mom to have found him a new home by now," Amy agreed, sitting back in her chair and watching Matt make his way back to their table with a loaded tray. "But the only people who looked at him didn't like his personality," Amy continued, making quote marks in the air. "That means he nipped at them, or he kicked at his stall while they were there. Or he just gave them a nasty look that scared them away." She threw up her hands in exasperation. "He hasn't had colic for ages. He'd do far better in a home with someone who could give him undivided attention. There are so many other horses at Heartland for me to concentrate on. I just can't give him the time he needs."

"Uh-oh." Soraya glanced towards the door. "Look out."

Matt put the tray down. "Not exactly the reception I expected," he said in a flat tone.

"I wasn't talking about you! Look who just walked in," Soraya muttered out of the corner of her mouth.

Amy let out a groan when she saw a tall girl with long, pale blonde hair stride purposefully towards them. Ashley Grant was in their year at school. She was a talented rider, and her parents could always afford to buy her the best horses. She lived at Green Briar, where her mom was also the trainer. Unlike Marion, Val Grant focused on top-level show horses. She wouldn't spend time rehabilitating an injured horse if there was no chance of it fulfilling its competitive potential.

Amy lowered her head and concentrated on cutting her cinnamon roll, but that didn't deter Ashley from standing over her with a rather scornful smirk on her face.

"Hello. I thought it was you guys I saw when I passed the window." She pulled her soft pink scarf away from her neck, letting her golden hair spill artfully over her shoulders.

"And you were right," Soraya said over-brightly. "What can we do for you?"

Ashley tossed her hair off her face, ignoring Soraya. "Are you entering the holiday show?" she asked Amy.

Amy sighed and let her fork clatter down on her plate as she looked up at Ashley. "Why? Are you worried?"

"About the Mule? I don't think so." Ashley laughed condescendingly.

Amy despised Ashley for having given Sundance such a hateful nickname, even if she herself found it rather

49

appropriate at times. However, given the current situation with the buckskin, Amy bit back her retort – even though Sundance had beaten Ashley and her prized pony in the last two competitions they had entered.

"What do you want, Ashley?" she asked pointedly.

"I thought you might be interested in knowing that we've just taken on a new horse, an incredibly talented showjumper named Blazing Glory."

"Congratulations," Amy said in a bored tone.

"Was that it?" Soraya leaned back in her chair and rolled her eyes at Matt, who flashed her a lopsided grin. "I feel like you always have some new flashy horse that you think is the best thing ever."

"Blazing Glory's owner is away for the holidays," Ashley continued as if Soraya hadn't spoken, "and she's asked me to ride him in the holiday show in the Large Pony Hunter division. Your classless pony really won't compare. He just doesn't have the breeding."

Amy knew that Ashley was trying to get to her, but she was determined not to reveal any of her anxieties about the competition as she flashed a smile at Ashley. "It must be wonderful to have a mother who lines up *well-bred* ponies for you to lose on," she said sweetly.

Soraya gave a snort of laughter.

"Keep laughing." Ashley flipped her scarf back over her shoulder. "We'll see who's smiling on December 26." She leaned over Matt's shoulder and scooped up a fingerful of icing from his plate. She licked it and then gave a deliberate smile. "If you keep eating that way, the Mule won't make it around the course anyway."

Without giving Amy the chance to come up with a smart reply, she turned on her heel and sauntered out of the café. They all watched her go.

"I don't know why she sets herself up like that. You're bound to beat her again," Matt said loyally, reaching over and giving Amy's arm a squeeze.

Amy smiled at him but her stomach was doing anxious somersaults. She couldn't share Matt's confidence in Sundance – not the way things were going lately.

Soraya met her eyes knowingly. "I'm sure Matt's right. You and Sundance are awesome together. By the time the show comes around, he'll be back on track and you'll prove that he's better than Ashley's push-button ponies any day."

Amy made an effort to join in her friends' laughter, but her heart wasn't in it. She didn't have a clue how she was going to get Sundance back in shape.

"Sorry, guys, but I've got to go," Matt said, looking at his watch. "I promised to meet my dad and help him choose a present for my mom. He always forgets what he bought her the year before."

"Thanks for the cinnamon roll," Amy said.

"No problem. And you don't need to worry about a few extra pounds, no matter what Ashley Grant might say," Matt told her with a consoling smile.

Amy's cheeks tingled as Soraya joked, "And you're not going to give me the same reassurance?"

"I don't think so. Your ego is big enough." Matt ruffled Soraya's hair as he left, calling over his shoulder, "Later!"

Soraya's eyes danced as she looked back to Amy. "Say, why don't we hit the stores again? You look like you need some retail therapy."

Amy pushed her plate away. When Matt had mentioned helping out his dad, she had remembered that her mom was at Heartland alone, since it was Ty's day off. "Do you mind if we do it some other time?" she said apologetically. "I need to get back and give my mom a hand. Ty's not working today and Grandpa is out running errands."

"Sure. Why don't I call you later and we can make plans to meet up later this week? Maybe we could catch a movie, too," Soraya said, reaching to lift her jacket off the back of the chair. "And don't forget we've got the party at Matt's on the twenty-third."

"Oh, don't worry. I'm not about to forget that," Amy said. She looked at her watch and figured that if she ran, she might be able to catch the next bus. She just hoped she would get home before her mom had finished all the chores on her own.

The yard was empty when Amy arrived back at Heartland. She dumped her bags inside the kitchen and reached up for her thick yard coat. It was freezing outside. It seemed as if the temperature had dropped and it was now cold enough for snow, but the clouds were grey and thin, not dense and dark.

"Mom?" she called, walking into the barn.

"In here," came the faint reply. Amy figured that her mom

was in the feed room and headed to the open door at the end of the aisle.

The sweet smell of sugar beet came from a line of buckets standing on the cracked flagstone floor.

"Did you get all your shopping done?" Marion put down the measuring spoon and turned to face Amy. Her face looked pale, and Amy felt a stab of concern as her mom began to massage her temples. She looked exhausted.

"Yeah, thanks. I came back to see if you need a hand with anything," Amy told her.

"That would be great. I'll need to bring the horses in from the fields soon, so if you could do that, it would be a big help." Marion screwed the lid back on to a giant tub of cod liver oil. "Hansel's owners came to pick him up today. They were really pleased with him."

"That's great," Amy said warmly. She felt happy for her mom, knowing how much joy she felt each time a horse left Heartland fully recovered. "I can start filling some hay nets," she offered, reaching up to take a handful of nets from the hook on the wall.

"Have you exercised Sundance?" said Marion. "He's looking restless, stuck in his stall. I won't be using the schooling ring again today, so you can have it to yourself."

"I'll do it after I fill the nets," Amy hedged. She was tired from her shopping trip, and the thought of tackling Sundance, who was feeling feisty by the sound of it, left her anxious.

"It will be dark if you wait much longer."

Marion spoke sharply and Amy looked up in surprise. It was

unlike her mom to snap. "Is everything OK?" she asked.

Marion sighed. "Sorry, hon. I'm just worn out, and I'm a little worried about Jake. He hasn't eaten for three days."

Amy frowned. That didn't sound like the elderly Clydesdale, a long-term Heartland resident, who usually attacked his feed bucket with huge enthusiasm, shaking his head from side to side as he searched out his favourite parts of the mix. She pictured the gentle giant that Marion had rescued from a horse sale a few years ago. "Have you tried any Bach Flower Remedies on him?" she asked.

Her mom nodded. "I've tried giving him some gorse, but he's not interested. I'm sure his arthritis is making him depressed, which is why he won't eat anything. It's not unusual in horses of his age when they feel their joints seizing up. I'm sure if I could get him to take the gorse, his depression would lift and his appetite would come back."

Amy thought of the way Jake hunted through his feed bucket, nosing around for the choicest bits. "This is probably going to sound silly," she said, "but have you thought about putting something extra tasty in his feed with the gorse to encourage him to eat? It might do the trick."

Marion stared and a smile spread slowly over her face. "No, I hadn't thought of that!" she exclaimed. "Thanks, Amy!"

"It might not work," Amy said, feeling overwhelmed by her mom's response.

"Yes, but it's still worth trying. I'll mix a cup of sunflower seeds into the bucket to see if that makes him more excited about his feed." Marion's voice rose with enthusiasm. "And if we can get him to eat, then I could put some chopped dandelion in, too, which is great for boosting appetite. Of course, he has to eat it first," she added with a short laugh.

Amy smiled to see her mom's spirits instantly improve. She was so invested in each and every one of the Heartland residents. They were all part of the family.

"I'll just go and take care of Sundance and then I'll be back to help you bring the horses in," Amy told her and headed for the tack room, feeling a thrill of pride that she'd been able to suggest a possible solution for Jake.

When she pulled back Sundance's stable door, the first thing the buckskin gelding did was lay his ears flat and snake his neck out. "Nice to see you, too," Amy muttered. She tried to slip the reins over his head and jumped back as Sundance stamped his foreleg close to her foot.

She glanced along the aisle and saw that the light beyond the open doors was already grey. By the time she managed to get Sundance tacked up, there would be very little daylight left to see where she was riding. Amy bit her lip. It would probably be best to turn him loose in the schooling ring again rather than try to ride him in the half-light. She needed to be fully alert in case he was in rare form again. She promised herself she would make time to ride him the next day.

She hung the bridle up on the hook just outside the door and took down the lead rope instead. Sundance watched her carefully. Amy could see how tense he was, his neck muscles taut as she gave him a quick pat. "Come on, silly," she said, snapping the lead rope on to his halter.

As she led him out the door, Sundance pulled forward, barging into Amy's shoulder and nearly tripping her. Amy bit back a shout of anger. Just what was wrong with him? None of the other horses took their problems out on her, and it wasn't like she treated them any differently.

She didn't want to stick around to watch Sundance after she had turned him out in the schooling ring. With a loud snort, the pony wheeled away from her with his hooves thudding on the sand. When he reached the top of the ring, he turned and raced back towards her with his ears back and the whites of his eyes showing. Amy slammed the gate as he skidded up to the fence, breathing heavily. She hurried back to the tack room to collect more halters and lead ropes before heading to the top field to begin bringing in the other horses.

When she walked past the schooling ring, Sundance had his head down and was muzzling the sand, showing no signs of the pent-up energy from only moments before. Amy was relieved to be able to focus on other horses for a short while.

Casper was already standing at the gate with his nose pointing comically upward, since he was too short to look over the fence properly. Jupiter, a seventeen-hand ex-racehorse, was standing alongside Casper. Amy smiled at the difference in their size. The two had formed a bond almost as soon as Casper arrived, and the diminutive grey pony was definitely the boss. Jupiter was so easygoing that he'd put up with almost anything. He was one of Amy's real favourites. Marion had rescued him after hearing that he was going to be auctioned for meat after a tendon injury ended his racing career. She was positive that she could find him a good home as a companion horse capable of going on trails and other light riding.

"Come on, boys," Amy said cheerfully, slipping through the gate and snapping on the lead ropes. "Dinner's about to be served."

There was a glassy chill in the air, and the horses' breath rose up in clouds as they made their way up to the yard. A bright light suddenly lit up the stable block, and Amy turned to see a yellow cab pulling up outside the kitchen door with its headlights on. She halted Jupiter and Casper and looked curiously to see who it could be.

A tall, slim figure stepped out of the back of the cab, pulling a hat further down over her ears. Amy peered more closely. It couldn't be Lou; she wasn't due to arrive until the next day.

There was an excited shout as the visitor caught sight of Amy and waved enthusiastically, calling her name.

Amy felt a rush of delight. There was no mistaking the clipped English accent. "Mom!" Amy cried in the direction of the feed room. "It's Lou. She's here!"

Chapter Five

"I'll just bring the rest of the horses in and then I'll be right back," Amy called excitedly as Marion ran out of the feed room, a huge smile stretched across her face. She led Jupiter and Casper around to the barn and settled them in their stalls before getting the others, including Sundance, who for once only halfheartedly tried to nip her hands as she unbuckled his halter.

When she finally let herself into the kitchen, Lou, Marion and Jack were sitting around the table with cups of coffee and a plate of cookies.

"Amy!" Lou got up and came over to give her a hug, enveloping her in a cloud of spicy perfume.

"Watch out, I'm a little grubby," Amy said quickly, conscious of Lou's immaculate cream slacks and pale blue shirt.

"Oh, don't worry," said Lou, taking a step back. "I dressed down for the flight."

Amy went over to the sink to wash her hands. "It's really good to see you," she said over her shoulder. "I thought you were arriving tomorrow."

"I decided to catch an earlier flight to surprise you all," Lou explained, sitting down at the table. "Carl had a meeting tonight, and I figured I'd only spend the evening in front of the TV. I had nothing else to do, considering I've been packed for a week, so I checked if I could change to an earlier flight and here I am!"

Amy diplomatically stayed away from the topic of her sister's boyfriend, Carl Anderson. She had only met him once a few months ago when Lou had invited her to New York City for the weekend. It was a short visit, but Amy hadn't liked Carl at all — the fact that he had laughed about Marion's work, calling her a horse shrink, certainly had not helped the two to become fast friends.

"I brought all the horses in. Jake took one sniff at his feed and dived in," she said to Marion, wiping her hands on a towel.

"You angel! That's marvellous," Marion said, her blue eyes sparkling.

"What's this about?" Jack asked.

Marion shared her worries about the Clydesdale, and how Amy had suggested using sunflower seeds to make his feed more tempting. Amy couldn't help noticing a bored expression settle on Lou's face as she began to examine her nails. Marion obviously noticed, too, because she quickly broke off what she was saying and asked, "Do we have any canned tomatoes, Dad? I know we have some meat in the fridge. I'll put together a quick shepherd's pie for dinner."

"My favourite." Lou stopped studying her fingernails and beamed as Jack got up to look in the pantry.

"Oh, I'm glad to hear that, Lou. I had your first meal all planned out, but I haven't had time to go to the store. That was on my list to do before you arrived tomorrow. So, it's good that the runner-up supper will do for now," Marion went on apologetically. "I had thought we could have a treacle sponge for your first dessert back home, something truly English since you probably don't get it much in the city, but—"

"Don't worry, Mom," Lou interrupted. "It's my fault for coming a day early. I don't really care what we eat. I just wanted it to be a surprise."

"It certainly was that," Jack said warmly, turning from the pantry, his eyes twinkling. "And luckily, your good old grandpa decided to pick up a cheesecake from the store today."

"Yum," said Lou, looking across at Amy and grinning. "It must be wonderful to have such great meals every day."

"We usually don't get the full works," Amy retorted, thinking about how her mom was normally out in the barn until late while Jack was often worn out after doing the one hundred and one odd jobs around the house. Amy realized too late that her comment might have come across as a criticism, but no one seemed to have noticed. Jack and Marion were both occupied pulling ingredients and cooking pans out of the cupboards.

"Can you clear the table, Amy, please?" Marion's voice was muffled as she rummaged around to find the biggest saucepan.

Amy scooped up an armful of magazines and a plastic grooming tray that was full of sponges. She had brought them inside the day before to rinse, preferring the warmth of the kitchen rather than freezing cold water from the spigot outside the barn.

"Here, let me help," said Lou, picking up a hoof pick and a snaffle bit. "I swear these were here the last time I visited," she teased. "Mom, you really should think about getting somebody in to help with the cleaning. You spend so much time looking after those horses that you don't have time to do anything else."

"Well, I help her. I cleaned out your room for you," Amy put in, knowing that she sounded hostile.

"Oh. You didn't have to do that," Lou said awkwardly.

"It was no problem. Amy had all of her things in your room. I wouldn't have known if she had stabled one of the horses in there, it was such a mess," Marion joked as she dumped a bag of potatoes on the counter. "Anyway, you know what to expect from us by now. Your room being cleaned was a special holiday treat. The house being cleaned wasn't even a consideration!"

Lou gave a faint smile as she put the hoof pick and bit on top of the bookshelf. Then she shouldered her bags that had been left by the door leading into the living room. "I'll just go get freshened up," she said.

Amy stayed in the kitchen to give her mom and grandpa a hand getting the meal ready. She thought about how Marion had laughed off her explanation of the state of the farmhouse, but Amy knew that her mother had wanted to get everything in better order before Lou arrived.

Lou's homecoming wasn't anything like Amy had hoped. Her mom seemed to be trying way too hard. Lou was part of the family, and this was the way they lived day to day. Why did they have to make such an effort for her?

Almost as if she sensed what Amy was thinking, Marion put down the potato peeler and said quietly, "I just want Lou's first night here to be special, OK? It's been so long since her last visit."

"Too long," Jack agreed, opening and dumping out a can of tomatoes. He rinsed out the empty can and looked at Amy, who was wiping down the counter. "We have to make the most of the short time that we have with her."

Amy nodded. She didn't want anything to spoil Lou's visit, either. Even though Lou had never been a constant presence in her life, she missed her sister between visits and wondered what it would have been like if they had grown up together. Amy resolved to concentrate on how good it was to be with Lou again.

"Mmm, this smells wonderful," Lou said appreciatively as Marion broke into the golden-topped pie to spoon a generous amount on to her plate.

"So," Jack said, blowing at a steaming forkful of pie, "what's in the box, honey?"

Lou had placed a round parcel, beautifully wrapped with silver and gold paper, in the centre of the table. "It's an early Christmas gift. I'll let you fight over who's going to open it," she said with a laugh.

Marion's blue eyes sparkled mischievously. "Well, since I made the pie, I think the honour should go to me."

"I took out the garbage," Jack protested, winking at Amy.

"And I brought in the horses." Amy joined in the fun.

"Well, I guess since none of us can decide, you'd better open it for us," Marion told Lou.

"Now?"

"Yes, or the anticipation will spoil my dessert!" Marion said, pushing the box across to Lou, who carefully pulled at the ribbons. She took off the lid and smiled broadly. "Look, it's a set of new Christmas decorations! I thought you could hang them on the tree," she explained, picking out a sparkling cut-glass icicle that had a loop of silver wire at one end. "They catch the light beautifully. I bought some for myself, too."

"Oh, Lou, they're gorgeous," Marion said, selecting one and holding it up to the light.

"Now all we need is a tree to put them on," Jack joked.

Lou raised an eyebrow. "You haven't got your tree up yet?"

"We always cut down a real one," Amy said, thinking that Lou's icicles might be a bit lost on the bushy evergreens they specially selected from the trails behind the stables each year. Although the icicles were beautiful, they would look out of place next to the colourful handmade wooden ornaments that Marion had picked up in Sweden when she had ridden in competitions there.

"Yes, they send me out into the wilderness with a saw and don't let me come home until I've cut down a beauty," Jack teased. He replanted three trees for every one that they cut down for firewood and for Christmas, he added, as if he were afraid Lou might think there'd be no trees bordering the trails in a few years.

Marion carefully laid the icicle back in the layers of tissue in the box and glanced at the clock on the mantelpiece. "I think I'll go check on Jake and see if he's finished his evening meal."

"I'll go if you want," Amy offered, wanting to give her mom the night off for once. "Why don't you come with me, Lou? I bet Pegasus would love to see you," she added.

"I doubt he'll remember me after all this time," Lou laughed. "If you don't mind, I think I'll stay in tonight. I'm feeling a bit tired, and I've always preferred a cosy kitchen to a draughty barn."

"OK," Amy said, unable to quell a surge of disappointment. Couldn't Lou see that she was trying to make an effort?

"It's nice of you to let Mom have some time to herself, though," Lou continued, looking across the table at Marion. "When was the last time you thought about pampering yourself a bit? I bet you can't even remember the last time you had your hair cut." She reached across and brushed the uneven fringe off her mother's forehead.

Marion shrugged with a rueful smile. "I like the natural look."

Amy pushed her chair back with a stab of frustration. Didn't Lou have anything supportive to say about their mom and the horses? "Living out here is not like being in the city where it's all about expensive clothes and high-powered office jobs," she blurted out.

"Hey! It's not just about that, however the movies might make it seem." Lou's eyes widened and then her tone softened. "I know how hard it is running a stable. Horses aren't new to me, you know." She took a deep breath and smiled. "I'd really like you to show me around in the morning."

"Sure," Amy said, taking her coat from the hook. She forced her shoulders to relax under the heavy waterproof fabric. "I'd like that, too."

The next morning Amy woke up early and decided to see to Sundance first thing so that another day wouldn't slip by without riding him. There were only a few days until the show, and she was determined not to let her mom down, or allow Ashley Grant to get the better of her after her cruel remarks in the mall café. The door to Lou's room was shut when Amy walked past it, so she figured her sister was sleeping in. She hoped they'd have time to walk around the yard later.

"Morning, sweetheart!" Marion called as she led Jupiter past Sundance's stall.

"Morning," Amy replied, warily reaching out to undo the straps on Sundance's stable blanket. To her relief, the gelding stood still. "Good boy," she said, folding back the rug and patting Sundance's neck. His golden ears flattened, and Amy braced herself for a sudden snap or kick, but Sundance kept his teeth and hooves to himself, and she was able to saddle and bridle him fairly easily.

"Are you going to be riding in the schooling ring?" Marion came back and leaned on the stall door. "I want to join up with Casper, but I don't mind waiting."

"You should go ahead. I thought I might take Sundance out for a trail ride before I use the arena," Amy told her.

"OK, just don't tire him out too much before your jumping session," her mom warned.

Amy suppressed a sarcastic laugh. Tire out Sundance? That would be the day!

She looped Sundance's reins over his head and clicked to him as she led the gelding out of his stall, down the aisle, and out on to the yard.

"Do you want me to hold him while you get on?" Hearing Sundance's clattering hooves, Ty appeared from one of the loose boxes.

"Thanks, but he seems to be on his best behaviour today," Amy said, swinging her leg over the saddle. Sundance shifted his weight and snorted. "I think he's looking forward to going out as much as I am."

"Have a good time," Ty called as Sundance turned away.

"We will!" Amy's spirits soared as she shortened her reins. It was so great that Sundance was cooperating at last. Maybe her hopes of having him going well by the time of the show weren't so far off the mark after all.

As soon as Sundance's hooves hit the sandy trail that led up Teak's Hill, the wooded slope that rose steeply behind Heartland, he broke into a canter. "Not yet," Amy told him, bringing him back to a trot. She felt Sundance tense underneath her, his stride turning choppy. *Oh, please don't start,* she thought, using her seat and hands to keep him collected. Sundance flattened his ears and snatched at the reins, giving Amy's arms a painful wrench. As her balance faltered, Sundance took advantage and burst into another canter. Amy fought to get him back under control, but he just extended his stride. He veered to the side of the track, and she had to duck to avoid the low-hanging branches. She tried to sit back in order to collect Sundance. She leaned back in the saddle and felt the pony's pace even out, but then he bolted to the side of the trail again.

This time, when she ducked to avoid the pine trees she wasn't fast enough, and a branch grazed her cheek with a fiery sting.

Sundance's canter became a gallop, and he sent stones bouncing away from underneath his hooves. His stride became so reckless that Amy was terrified he would stumble and fall. She braced one of the reins over his neck while giving and taking with the other, just as her mother had taught her. The gelding finally began to check his pace until Amy had enough control to circle him. Her stomach twisting in knots, she brought him to a shaky halt.

Sundance dropped his head. His flanks were covered with sweat, heaving in and out with raspy breaths. "OK, that's it. We're going home," Amy said out loud, shortening her reins. She felt winded and jolted as they headed back down the path. Sundance was quieter now that he had spent his spare energy, but Amy had had enough. She slipped off him as soon as they were back on the yard, feeling her legs wobble. "Walk on," she said curtly, leading him back to his stall and unbuckling his saddle and bridle. She picked up a wisp to rub Sundance down, and with no warning, he swung his head around and nipped her side.

"Ow!" Amy exclaimed, wincing. She glared at the gelding as he laid his ears back.

"Is everything OK?" said Ty. His footsteps hurried up the aisle and he looked over the door.

"He just bit me." To her horror, Amy felt tears filling her eyes, and she blinked them back furiously.

"Why don't you let me rub him down?" Ty offered.

"Thanks." Amy's throat was stinging as she left the stable, thrusting the wisp into Ty's hands. At least he had been tactful enough not to mention how soon she had come back from her ride. In a way, his sympathetic offer to help made her feel even worse. Ty shouldn't have to cool down Sundance or tack him up, but he was always willing to help, and Amy didn't exactly enjoy spending a lot of time with the crankiest pony in the world. Amy felt like she was failing everyone – especially Sundance. And yet, she was sure that it was the pony's own fault.

Amy was hurrying towards the house when a friendly nicker caught her attention.

"Pegasus!" Amy turned towards the big, grey gelding who was watching her over his stall door with his ears pricked. Without thinking twice, she pulled back the bolt on the door and slipped inside. No matter what went wrong, Pegasus was always there, gentle and understanding. The gelding lipped at the top of Amy's head when she turned her face into his mane and replayed Sundance's uncontrolled gallop in her mind. She couldn't remember ever feeling such a sense of despair about a horse. She didn't know how much longer she could deal with Sundance's unpredictability. Why couldn't she connect with him? Marion always seemed to build bonds with the problem horses that arrived on the yard. Amy had spent a lot of time riding Sundance, and still there was no understanding between them.

"Hey." Ty's voice broke into Amy's thoughts. She lifted her head and saw him leaning over the door. "Are you OK? What happened?"

"Nothing," Amy said, forcing a smile. "I'm fine, really. Sundance has sharp teeth, that's all."

Ty raised his eyebrow. "Yeah? I don't think that's it. Something's up." He looked straight at her. "Come on, you can tell me."

Amy felt a surge of frustration. "Tell you what? I don't know what's wrong with him!"

"Then that's a good reason to talk about it," he retorted.

Amy looked down and twisted a strand of Pegasus's mane around her finger. "The way you saw Sundance behaving the other day in the schooling ring, well, that wasn't unusual. He's been like that for a few weeks. I just don't know why he's doing it. It's like he hates me." She broke off miserably.

"Come on, you know that's not true. He's like that with everyone. And you know how to get the best out of him. He does better for you than anyone else. I mean, look at the summer shows."

"That feels like it was years ago," Amy said gloomily. "I just can't get through to him any more. It's like he wants to be bad."

"I don't think your mom would agree that any horse *wants* to be bad," Ty pointed out. "Have you talked to her about this?"

"I don't want to," Amy said quickly. "At least, not yet. Not with Lou here. I don't want to do anything to spoil her visit. I'll talk to her about it after Lou's gone, I promise," she added as Ty looked sceptical.

She patted Pegasus on the shoulder while Ty opened the door to let them out. "Thanks for listening," she said.

"No problem," he said, then hesitated. "Amy, your mom would

want to know you're having difficulties with Sundance. She wouldn't want you to wait until something goes really wrong."

Amy felt a flash of annoyance. She knew deep down that Ty was making sense, but why did he have to butt in? If she told her mom, she'd have to tell her everything — including the fact that she hadn't been giving Sundance enough attention lately; that she'd started to give up on him as soon as things started to go wrong.

"She wants you to do well in the show to give him the chance of finding a good home," Ty added.

Before she could stop herself, Amy turned on Ty, raising her voice. "Like you said, I've already won two blue ribbons with him! If he wasn't such a nasty pony, that would have been more than enough to get him sold."

Ty's eyebrows shot up in surprise at Amy's attack, but she couldn't resist one final comment. "I feel sorry for whoever ends up with him. I really do."

Chapter Six

Amy tucked her feet up and wriggled further back into the chair, away from the draught coming from the open door.

"It's one heck of a cold morning out there," said Jack, rubbing his hands together as he came in from outside.

"Did you have enough sand to get to the end of the driveway?" Marion asked, spreading some butter on a fresh piece of toast.

"Yes, and it was good timing. Look who I found trying to make his way up to the house," Jack said, standing aside to let Scott Trewin, Matt's older brother, walk into the room.

"I hit a patch of black ice at the bottom of the drive, and my Jeep ended up with the headlights pointing straight into a ditch," Scott admitted. "There was no way I was going anywhere until Jack appeared with his trusty shovel!" He put down a package wrapped in brown paper on the table. "Here are the antibiotics you needed, and the veterinary magazines I promised you," he said to Marion, who was handing a piece of toast to Amy.

"Wonderful! Thank you. I look forward to wading my way through those," Marion said, offering Scott the plate of toast.

"Thanks," he said. "I didn't have a chance to grab anything for breakfast since I got called out early."

"Was it an emergency?" asked Jack, pouring out four coffees.

"Well, it was made out to be one when the owner phoned

the clinic, but when I arrived at the yard, there wasn't much of a situation to deal with," Scott said, sitting down at the table and running his hand through his dark hair.

"False alarm?" Marion suggested, sitting opposite him.

Scott sighed. "Not really. Would you believe it was someone wanting me to give them a vet's signature for auction? They're selling a dressage horse that's clearly lame, and they wanted me to sign for a clean bill of health. He actually hinted at a bribe."

"Where was this?" Marion asked.

Scott told them the stable name and Amy leaned forward out of her chair, realizing that it was the same yard she had visited with her mother a few days earlier.

"The horse wasn't named Rising Star, was it?" Marion questioned.

Scott looked puzzled. "No, that wasn't the name. Do you know the stable?"

"We visited recently."

A faint memory drifted into Amy's mind, and she felt her stomach twist. "Was it a black mare, by any chance? Maybe an Arabian?"

Scott nodded. "Yes, that sounds like the one. She's been overworked, probably for several months. And the sand in their arena looked deep, which is more than enough to make a sensitive horse lame on her front legs." Scott looked from Amy to Marion. "She's developed windgalls, too. It'll take her weeks of stable rest to recover. The owners want to get rid of her, but still want the price of a sound dressage horse." He took the cup of coffee that Jack was holding out and sipped at it gratefully.

"You didn't sign the papers, did you?" Amy stood up, her voice rising with anxiety.

"No, of course not." Scott shook his head. "But I'm afraid that's not going to stop them from sending her over to the auction house in town today. You don't really need vet papers. They just thought it would ensure the sale."

Amy stared at Scott in alarm. "But that's no good if she's sold to someone who expects a healthy horse. It'll take a lot to get her well. The new owner might get fed up with a lame horse and put her down! Or if she's really that lame," her mind raced, "she could go for meat! Mom!" She shot a panicked glance at Marion, whose mouth had settled into a tight line.

"Morning, all!" Lou strode into the kitchen fully dressed, her eyes bright and her hair done. "Who's for crepes? Orange and chocolate is my speciality." She glanced at Scott at the table and smiled. "Hello there."

"Lou, this is Scott Trewin, our vet. Scott, this is my granddaughter Lou." Jack introduced them.

Despite the niceties, Lou's eyes were drawn to Marion, who was drumming her fingers on the table, a distracted expression clouding her eyes.

"Oh, there's nothing wrong with one of the horses, is there?" Lou asked.

Scott shook his head at the same time as Amy said, "Yes!"

Lou looked confused. "Well, which is it?"

"There is a horse in trouble, but it's not one of ours," Amy said impatiently.

"Not yet," Marion said grimly. She pushed her chair away from the table and went over to the bookcase. Amy felt a surge of hopeful expectation as her mom reached for the phone directory and began flipping through the pages.

"What are you looking for?" Amy asked.

"The auction house. I want to see what time their sale is today," Marion told her. She glanced at Jack. "I might have to be out for a while. Do you have time to give Ty a hand if he needs it?"

Jack nodded. "I was going to get the tree, but that can wait."

"I'd better get going. My morning appointments start in twenty minutes," Scott said. "Thanks for the coffee, and let me know how it all turns out."

"Will do," said Marion, picking up the phone. "Thanks, Scott."

"Don't mention it." He looked keenly at Marion for a moment. "I had a feeling you might do something like this. Good luck."

Scott and Jack left at the same time, leaving Amy and Lou listening to Marion, who had got through to the auction house.

"Right, thank you," she said, before hanging up and turning to face them. "The sale starts at one o'clock, and they open in half an hour for presale viewing. They have a dressage pony registered under the name of Princess Jasmine. That sound right?" She looked at Amy, who gave her a nod, then began to hunt around the room. "Car keys, car keys," she muttered.

"They're in your coat pocket. Here." Amy tossed her mom's coat to her while shrugging into her own.

Lou looked from one to the other with a bemused expression. "What are you doing?"

"We're going to be gone for an hour or so. Will you be OK?" Marion asked.

"Sure, I'd just like to know what's going on. Can I help?"

Amy pulled on her boots while Marion quickly told Lou about Jasmine's plight.

Lou looked surprised. "Is it really necessary for you to get involved? I'm sure that the pony will find a good home. I mean, people looking at her will realize that she's lame, so if they buy her, it will be because they plan to nurse her back to health, won't it?"

"The reason she's going to auction is because there's a good chance someone will buy her there without noticing the lameness." Amy felt a surge of impatience with her sister's apparent lack of concern.

"And there's a very good chance that somewhere down the line, she'll end up being put down," Marion added.

"Well, I wish you luck, but don't do anything hasty," Lou said, picking up the coffee pot and pouring herself a cup.

Amy shot a frustrated glance at her mom, thinking how little empathy Lou had for what they did at Heartland. But Marion wasn't looking.

"Aren't we going to take the trailer?" Amy asked, following her mom outside and climbing into the car beside her.

She shook her head. "Ty's car is in the way, and we don't have time to find him to get it moved."

She pressed down on the accelerator, careful to stay on the

gritted trail that Jack had put down. Amy could sense how tense her mom was, and her own stomach was tying itself in knots. She couldn't get the picture of the pretty, dish-faced black mare out of her mind.

"I don't get how people can treat animals in such a callous way," she burst out, once her mom had negotiated her way down the drive and joined the main road. "It's totally wrong."

Marion nodded, keeping her eyes fixed on the road ahead. "Some people don't deserve to own animals. It is a privilege, especially when you consider how much love animals offer in return. When you own a horse, whether it's for pleasure or for show, it has to be a two-way relationship, giving *and* taking on both parts."

Amy nodded. She was so proud of her mom and how she always took time out to help a horse she knew was in trouble, no matter how chaotic things were at Heartland.

The roads were much clearer than usual, with few people wanting to venture out in the icy conditions. Marion turned the car heater on full blast and drummed her hands impatiently against the steering wheel when the lights ahead turned red.

"What happens if we get there and Jasmine has already been sold?" Amy dared to ask the question that she couldn't get out of her mind.

"We'll cross that bridge if and when we come to it," Marion said grimly, letting out the clutch and accelerating away as the lights turned green.

When they pulled into the auction house parking lot, Amy's heart sank. She had hoped that the bad weather would have deterred people from attending the sale, but the lot was nearly full. And the large, low-roofed building, divided into scores of pens, was already crowded with people, even though the bidding wasn't due to start for another twenty minutes.

Marion disappeared to get an auction catalogue, leaving Amy to walk along the metal-railed pens. She ran her eyes over the rows of horses and ponies, looking for the black mare. She was suddenly jolted back to the last time they had been at an auction house, when she had come across a buckskin gelding, snapping and kicking out at anyone who came too near. How could it be that six months later, Sundance still wasn't behaving any better? He was well cared for and fed, but he still had the attitude of a neglected pony. Amy pressed her hand against her stomach, feeling queasy as she reminded herself that at least Sundance was infinitely better off where he was now, compared with where he might have ended up. For that same reason, they needed to take Princess Jasmine back to Heartland that day.

Marion came up beside her. "Follow me," she said, "I got Jasmine's sale number." She plunged into the press of people peering over the rails or standing in small groups discussing livestock. The buzz of conversation was surprisingly loud.

"Here!" Marion called, pulling up abruptly and squeezing past three men, two of whom were wearing thick waterproof parkas and wool hats. Amy recognized the third man immediately. Tapping a rolled-up auction guide against his hand was the same person who had been shouting commands at the girl riding Jasmine. The black mare was in front of them, her head hung low and her eyes half closed.

"I think that's Jasmine's owner," Amy said in a low voice. Her mom glanced over her shoulder at the group of laughing men and narrowed her eyes. Then she looked back at Jasmine.

"It's like she knows exactly what's happening," Amy said quietly. "She isn't even interested in looking at anyone."

Marion held her hand through the bars and clicked encouragingly. "Come on, Jasmine, there's a good girl." But the pony didn't even flicker an ear in her direction.

"She was nothing like this the other day," Amy said. "She was obviously sore on her forelegs, but apart from that she seemed fine. And she was trying really hard to please her rider."

"You don't have to convince me," Marion told her. She kneeled down to get a better look at the mare's front legs. Amy bent down as well.

"It looks like the swelling has gone down. He might have given her an anti-inflammatory, which would help explain her listless nature. Well, here goes," Marion said, standing up and then turning around to face the men. "Am I right that one of you gentlemen is the owner of this pony?" she asked briskly.

"That's right. I'm Josh Williams." The large man with the florid complexion stepped forward and offered his hand.

"Mr Williams, my name is Marion Fleming." Amy's mom shook the outstretched hand just once before dropping it. "I'm interested in buying your pony, and I'm prepared to pay extra if you withdraw her from the auction and sell her to me now." She named a figure that Amy noticed was far more than the minimum listed in the catalogue.

"Oh." Josh Williams looked taken aback. "I'm sorry, but

you're too late. I've already agreed on a sale with this gentleman." He indicated the fair-headed man standing next to him.

"Is that so?" Marion asked, her voice calm.

Amy knew her mom better than to think she would give up without a fight, but her stomach was still tying itself in knots as she reached her hand into the pen to smooth Jasmine's neck. "Hang in there, sweetheart. Everything's going to be OK," she whispered, her heart racing.

"And you would be?" Marion turned to the other man with her most disarming smile. He had a kind expression, but he did not seem like an auction-house regular. His coat looked too new, and he was wearing loafers with thin rubber soles. Amy thought he didn't look like much of a horseman.

"I'm the new owner of Princess Jasmine," the man told her, grinning around at the other men. "As soon as the lawyer comes around to approve the sale, my friend and I are loading up Princess Jasmine to surprise my daughter as a Christmas present."

"Really?" Marion asked with an outward sigh. "That sounds very nice, but I hope you know that this pony is lame, and she is in no shape to be ridden for several weeks, maybe months." She went on, still smiling pleasantly. "I don't want to discourage you from buying your daughter a pony, but this one will need exceptional care and the supervision of a vet."

The man frowned and looked from Marion to his friend, to Mr Williams.

"No, I don't know about any lameness," he confessed. "I just want a good starter pony. My daughter just started dressage lessons last year."

"Well, this pony is sore on both forelegs because she has been overschooled. My daughter and I saw her working less than a week ago."

Amy was starting to feel a little nervous. Her mom's voice was so confident, but Amy could see how the men were eyeing her suspiciously.

The fair-headed man turned to Mr Williams, whose cocky grin had turned to a seething scowl.

"She only needs a short rest," he blurted out. "I've had that confirmed by the vet who's overseeing the auction. The mare'll be back in top form then. She's a champion in the making." But before he'd even finished, the other man and his companion were walking away, shaking their heads in disgust.

Josh Williams stepped up close to Marion. "You've just lost me a sale. I hope you have a good lawyer! People who make false accusations should have deep pockets."

Amy felt her palms grow clammy, and she glanced nervously at her mother.

"I don't think we'll be needing a lawyer. I made you my offer," Marion told Mr Williams, her voice dangerously low. Her head barely reached his shoulder, but she stood in front of him without flinching. "And you might like to reconsider the description 'false'. I happen to know this mare is not only lame, but that there is absolutely no guarantee that she will ever be up to the strenuous training that any top dressage pony needs."

"How..." Josh Williams began, but Marion wasn't through. She raised her hand in the air.

"I'm a good judge of horses — better than your last prospective buyer, that's for sure. Now, let me make myself clear. I am not leaving until I buy your pony. The price I've offered is more than fair. If you think that you're going to put her through the auction in the hope that someone else who doesn't know a good horse from a lame one will buy her, then I suggest you think again, because I will be standing on the sidelines proclaiming to the entire auction house that this horse will not be fit to be worked for a long, long time."

Amy couldn't take her gaze off her mom. Marion's head was thrown back and her eyes were flashing dangerously. The way she looked, Amy could well imagine her mother doing just what she threatened. By now, the small clusters of people examining nearby horses were all looking at Marion. Amy felt herself blush, knowing her mom had made such a commotion, but Marion Fleming was not yet finished.

"And finally, Mr Williams," Marion continued, enunciating each word, "if you refuse my offer, then I will make things very difficult for you at the boarding stable where you and your daughter currently keep your horse. And I know the owners of many boarding stables in this area. Once the trainers find out how you find ponies dispensable, I have a feeling that you will have very few friends in the riding community. Very few friends indeed."

Amy glanced around to see that the onlookers were now all

focused on Mr Williams. They shook their heads before heading on their way.

Mr Williams was already holding out his hand for the cheque that Marion was beginning to write. Amy opened the door to Jasmine's pen, and slipped inside. She looked over to see Marion handing the check to Mr Williams. Amy felt flushed with relief. She placed her arms around the mare's warm neck.

"You're coming back with us," she whispered to Jasmine. "You're coming home to Heartland."

Chapter Seven

"Now what?" Amy looked at Marion as they stood in the parking lot with Jasmine standing between them. The wind was picking up, and Amy noticed that the mare was shivering.

"I don't know. I didn't think past getting Mr Williams to accept my cheque," Marion confessed. She caught Amy's eye, and they both burst into laughter. In between gasps, Marion explained, "Actually, I phoned Dad when I was signing the papers for Jasmine. He should be here any minute with the trailer." She wiped her fingers under her eyes, where laughter and the cold had filled them with tears.

"Mom, you were pretty impressive," Amy told her, rubbing Jasmine's nose. The black mare was looking warily around her unfamiliar surroundings, her delicate Arabian ears pricking at each voice and engine passing by.

"Oh, I don't know. I don't think those are the words Mr Williams would have used," Marion said more soberly. "I was just so angry at what he was doing." She pulled Jasmine's forelock out from under her halter and smiled. "But all's well that ends well, as Shakespeare would say."

"I'll admit, I was getting worried when you started making threats. Do you really think you could have convinced stable owners not to board his horses?"

Marion shrugged modestly. "I didn't have time to think

about what I was saying. I'm sure there are stables that wouldn't think what he was doing was wrong."

"Yeah, like Green Briar," Amy offered.

"Well, thank goodness we'll never get the chance to find out. Hey, here's Dad!"

Amy handed Jasmine's lead rope to her mother and waved with both arms towards the trailer pulling into the parking lot.

"Honestly, I can't leave you two alone for a second," Jack called through the open window. He left the motor running and jumped out beside them. "You were just like this when you were younger, Marion. You'd go out to play and come back with a different stray animal every time."

"Dad!" Marion protested, as Jack gave Amy a wink on his way around to the back of the trailer.

"I brought a blanket for the pony," he explained when Amy joined him and helped to tug back the bolts. They lowered the ramp, and she saw the blanket thrown over the partition divider. "I think it might be a little big," he added.

"That's OK. Anything to throw over her will be great. She's shivering, and she doesn't have much of a winter coat," Amy said.

Marion led Jasmine around to them and encouraged her up the ramp. The mare walked into the trailer without hesitating and stood patiently while Amy buckled the blanket in place.

"Amy can travel with you and I'll follow behind in the car," Marion told Jack, once the ramp was firmly secured back into place.

Throughout the journey home, Amy kept a constant eye on

Jasmine through the window between the truck cab and the trailer. The mare spent most of the time with her eyes half closed, swaying with the motion of the truck.

"I wish I could tell her that she's going to be OK now," Amy sighed. "You should have seen her in the auction house, Grandpa. She looked as if she'd given up on everything and everyone."

"Marion will help her out," Grandpa said confidently, switching on the radio. "I've never met a horse that she hasn't been able to reach." He began tapping his thumb in time to the Christmas song playing on the radio. "Sleigh bells ring, are you listening?"

Amy laughed out loud, suddenly filled with hope. "Merry Christmas, Jaz!" she called to the pony through the window, before joining in the song herself.

It was long past lunchtime, but Amy and Marion wanted to settle Jasmine in before thinking about food for themselves. Amy watched her mom sort out the various remedies she was going to use to treat the mare. Ty was with Jasmine, putting down an extra-thick bed of straw in her stall.

"What are you going to use this for?" Amy asked, picking up a bottle of arnica tincture.

"That treats swelling and joint inflammation," Marion explained. "You can prepare it if you like. It needs to be diluted one part tincture to two parts water. There's a bowl in the cupboard and clean rags. We'll need to soak them in the tincture and wrap them around Jasmine's legs."

"OK," said Amy. She filled up and clicked on the self-heating kettle, which stood on a table in the corner of the room, and went to rummage around in the old metal cupboard.

When the treatment was ready, she carried the steaming bowl into the barn to join her mom and Ty. Jasmine gave a low nicker when she saw Amy approach.

"Sorry, girl, it's nothing nice to eat," Amy told her, placing the bowl on the floor well away from the mare's hooves.

"She's sweet," Ty said as Jasmine rested her head against his shoulder. "I'm glad you bought her."

"Hold her steady, Ty, she might want to shift around a little," Marion warned, rolling up her sleeves. She squeezed out the cloth from the bowl and wrapped it carefully around Jasmine's legs.

"OK, girl, OK," Amy murmured, joining Ty on the other side of the mare's head when she tried to step away from Marion's hands.

Marion held the cloth against Jasmine's leg, giving the liquid time to soak into her swollen joints before neatly bandaging the cloth in place. She did the whole process again for the other leg before straightening up.

"She has articular windgalls," Marion explained, "which is when excess fluid collects in the fetlock joint."

Ty frowned. "I thought windgalls were harmless."

Amy's mom nodded. "Yes, but we should recognize them as a warning sign, so Jasmine needs lots of rest. She has to stay in the stall for the first week she's here, so we can avoid any further damage to her legs." She patted Jasmine's shoulder.

"We'll get Scott to come and take another look at her to be on the safe side, but in the meantime, I'm going to start her on some Bach Flower Remedies. We'll want to treat her emotionally as well as physically. Ty, what remedies would you suggest?"

He thought for a moment. "Larch to start with," he said at last. "I think she could use a confidence boost."

"Good idea," Marion agreed. "Larch will reduce fear of failure, too, which Jasmine will be feeling after being rejected by her owner. Plus we can give her aspen, which is good for reducing anxiety."

Amy didn't usually get involved in the healing part of her mom's work. She loved to ride, but Marion and Ty tended to decide on the treatments while she was at school. But now she felt a stirring of interest in the remedies that would be used to help bring Jasmine back to full health.

"The other Bach Flower Remedy I'd like to try is one I haven't shown you before. In fact, I don't even think I've got it written down in my books," Marion said. Amy knew that her mom kept detailed notes on her research in the desk in the tack room. "It's called century, and it helps rebuild self-esteem, which sounds pretty unusual for a horse, I know."

"Really?" Amy said, curious. She hadn't realized that remedies could do that sort of thing.

Marion nodded. "Over a period of time, it will help Jasmine to develop her own sense of self-worth, rather than relying on what she gets from outside stimuli, like the people who handle her," Marion explained.

Amy couldn't help thinking about Sundance while her mom was talking. Maybe it would be worth asking her mom about treatments for his behavioural problems. But then she pushed the thought away again. The only reason the gelding was being difficult was because he was stubborn. Marion had already treated him for his behavioural problems as well as the malnutrition he suffered from his previous home. The pony was just plain moody, and nothing could cure that, she was sure.

After they had left Jasmine a bucket of water with the remedies carefully added, the three went inside in search of food. Jack had gone out to buy some extra sand in case it snowed, so only Lou was at home. She looked up from the book she was reading, curled in a comfy armchair in the corner of the kitchen.

"How did it go?" she asked, getting up and filling the kettle. "You bought the pony, then?"

"Yes, we got there in the nick of time, thank goodness," Marion glanced at the bare table. "Um, do you know what we've got for lunch? These guys must be starving. I know I am."

"I thought we could order pizza. My treat," said Lou, stretching her arms into the air and yawning.

Amy felt her stomach growl, and she looked at the clock. It was half past two, and hours since breakfast. "We live too far out of town for home delivery," she said shortly. She couldn't believe that Lou hadn't thought they might all want something to eat as soon as they came in! She pulled off her coat and scarf, forcing herself to swallow her harsher words – she knew

Marion couldn't stand petty arguments, especially not between her daughters, who rarely saw each other.

"It's not a problem. I'll throw together some scrambled eggs," Marion said. "Amy, maybe you could do a fruit salad."

"Sorry," Lou said mildly. "I should have realized that it's not as easy as New York here."

"You've got that right," Amy muttered under her breath.

Ty was pulling his boots off alongside her, and he raised his eyebrows questioningly, but Amy didn't say anything else. She just rolled her eyes and went over to the sink to wash her hands.

"Would you like to see what I've been up to?" Lou asked, over the sound of Marion breaking eggs into a bowl. "I know you've been busy with the new horse – and I'm really glad you bought her, by the way – but I've not exactly been idle myself."

"Sure, let's see," Ty answered with his easy smile.

Lou left the room and returned moments later carrying a huge Christmas wreath made of evergreen branches twisted into a circle. "Do you like it? It took ages to make, but I thought it would add some real festive spirit if we hung it on the back door," she said, reshaping one of the red ribbons that had been hidden by the holly leaves. Her cheeks were flushed, and she sounded very pleased with her morning's work. "My friends in England always had one of these at Christmas, and I thought it would remind us all of home. I mean..." She broke off, looking flustered.

"It's gorgeous," Marion said smoothly from where she was

scraping the spatula through the eggs on the stove. "That was really thoughtful, Lou."

"Too bad it's not edible," Amy said under her breath, as she clattered a pile of cutlery down on the table. Too late, she realized that her sister had overheard her.

Lou's cheeks burned a deep shade of pink. "Look, I'll go get some easy-cook meals from the store tomorrow. Or I can go when Grandpa is back with the car. It would be a good idea for you to be stocked up on them anyway, since you spend so much time on the yard. Those horses eat better than you do!"

"Thank you, yes," Marion said quickly, with a warning glance at Amy, who had a much sharper reply on the tip of her tongue. She lifted the eggs off the stove. "These are just about done, so Ty, if you can grab some plates we can all eat."

Ty lifted the china out of the cupboard and Marion served up the hasty lunch. Amy took a mouthful of fluffy scrambled eggs, and as her hunger eased, she began to feel bad about her earlier remark. After all, Lou had sounded like she was pleased they'd managed to save Jasmine. Amy looked across at her. "Would you like to come out with me and see Jasmine after lunch?" she suggested.

"Well…" Lou began with such hesitation that Amy was sure she would refuse, but then Lou smiled. "That would be great," she said warmly.

Amy caught the relieved expression on her mom's face, and she felt glad that she had made the effort to make Lou feel included.

"I'll see you outside," Ty said, pushing back his chair.

"I'm going to lunge Sundance. Thanks for lunch."

With an uneasy jolt, Amy guessed that Ty was doing this to help her out. She glanced up as he walked past and he gave her a quick smile. Amy thought, not for the first time, what a nice guy Ty was. He didn't seem to be letting any bad feelings linger since she had snapped at him yesterday. She scraped up the last of the eggs, and Marion insisted on washing the dishes so Amy could take Lou down to the barns.

"Thanks, Mom," said Amy, carrying her plate over to the sink before heading for the door. She wound her scarf tightly around her neck and noticed that Lou was pulling the zipper on her jacket all the way up to her chin. "Good idea, it's really cold out," Amy said, opening the door. "Be careful to stay on the sandy areas," she warned, pointing to the various trails scattered across the yard.

"Thanks," said Lou, crunching across the gritty surface.

Amy led the way past the stable block and around to the barn. Sundance looked over his door when they walked in and watched them make their way up the centre aisle. "Which one is this?" Lou asked, stopping just in front of him.

"Sundance. He's the one Ty is going to lunge. He was here the last time you came, but he was really new and was still sick with colic," Amy told her. "He's much better now. We're hoping to be able to place him with some new owners soon."

"Hello, boy," said Lou, and before Amy could stop her, she stretched out her hand to the gelding.

Sundance laid his ears back and rolled his eyes as he nipped at Lou's hand, his teeth just grazing the finger of her glove before she snatched it away.

"Are you OK?" Amy gasped in dismay. Lou's face had drained of colour.

"I'm fine," she replied shortly, tucking her hand under her arm. "It was just a bit of a shock."

"Sundance is one of our more unpredictable guests," Ty said, coming up behind them with a lunge line.

"I'd say that was an understatement. I thought it was only the English who did that," Lou wrinkled her nose and stood back for Ty to open the door to Sundance's stall.

"Come on, Jaz is in the end stall," Amy said, impatient to leave the bad-tempered buckskin behind and show Lou the latest Heartland arrival.

When they looked over the door, she was pleased to see that Jasmine was lying down with her legs tucked under her stomach. Her eyes were closed and her head nodded slightly as she dozed.

"She seems sweet." Lou kept her voice low.

Amy pointed to the hint of white bandage on Jasmine's forelegs. "Mom's treated the swelling in her legs, and hopefully, if Jaz rests for a while, she can be brought back into light work." She shrugged. "We may even be able to rehome her one day if we find the right owners."

"Uh-huh," Lou said. She fiddled with the bolt on Jasmine's door. "You know, you're starting to sound just like Mom." She looked up and smiled. "It must be rubbing off on you, all the time you spend here."

Amy felt taken aback, especially since she was just realizing how little of the healing side of the business she knew. "I guess I just want to see Jasmine recover so she's able to have a good, easy life," she said. "She seems to have such a generous nature."

Lou's eyebrows rose. "You make it sound like she's a person."

Amy couldn't figure out if her sister was laughing at her. Of course she treated the horses like they each had their own personalities. "Would you like to see the new schooling ring?"

"OK," said Lou, turning to leave without a backward glance at Jasmine.

Amy pointed out the arena as they walked down the path leading away from the barn. "We use it for schooling, but it was specially designed for join-up," she explained. "It's more of a circle than a rectangle, see?"

"Mmm," Lou replied, but her blonde hair swung forward as she looked at the ground, and she seemed more concerned with where she was putting her feet than anything else.

They leaned on the gate of the arena to watch Ty working Sundance on the lunge. "He's going really well," he called. "Do you want to get on and ride him around a few times?"

Amy looked at Sundance, who was cantering steadily around the ring with the saddle and bridle on, his head proudly arched. He had a calm rhythm that reminded Amy of their success over the summer, and she let her expectations rise. "Do you mind?" She turned to Lou. "I'll only ride him around a couple of times."

Lou shrugged. "Go ahead."

Amy jogged across the sand and borrowed Ty's helmet

before accepting a leg up. Sundance stood perfectly still as she adjusted her chin strap. "I'll just take him around twice," she said, shortening the reins and clicking to the gelding.

Sundance hesitated at first, stiffening in every muscle, and then shot forward. "Steady," Amy gasped, bringing him back to a trot and guiding him around the perimeter of the ring. He soon found his pace and settled on the bit, and Amy allowed herself to relax a little.

"Do you want to try him over the fence?" Ty called. He had set up a low jump in the centre of the ring.

Amy trotted another circuit and then turned Sundance up the middle of the ring. The gelding's pace was smooth, and Amy enjoyed his strong, even paces. But three strides away from the jump, Sundance thrust up his head and swerved sideways. Amy was caught totally off guard as he stretched his neck forward and threw himself over the fence. Amy fell on to his neck, and then Sundance surged into a full gallop and headed for the entrance gate.

"No!" she yelled, pulling on the reins. She knew that Sundance was perfectly capable of clearing the gate, but there was a sheet of ice on the opposite side. And Lou was standing nearby, frozen with shock.

Amy couldn't anticipate what Sundance would do, so she sat back in the saddle and pulled with all her might.

"Sundance, will you listen?" she gasped and tried one final time to slow him down, knowing that if he didn't respond she would have to prepare to jump right out of the arena. But something in Amy's voice seemed to get through to the gelding, and he choppily changed his stride and skidded to a halt with his nose touching the top bar of the gate.

Amy met Lou's startled gaze and groaned inwardly, knowing how that spectacle would not help Lou warm to Sundance or any of the other Heartland horses. "Lou," she began, but her sister had already turned and headed up the path without saying a word.

"Great," Amy sighed, sliding off Sundance's back.

"I'm sorry, I shouldn't have suggested that you take the jump. Are you OK?" Ty said as he joined her.

"I'm fine," Amy told him. After this episode, she was more angry than scared. "I'd better go after Lou. Can you cool Sundance down?" she asked, handing Ty the reins.

"Sure." Ty pushed his dark hair out of his eyes and frowned at Sundance. "What is the problem with you?"

That was a question that Amy couldn't answer. She decided that enough was enough. She was going to have to tell her mom about the way Sundance was behaving. But she forgot all thoughts of Sundance when she reached the barn and heard the clatter of hooves on concrete. Amy's heart skipped a beat when she saw Jasmine heading straight towards her at a wild trot.

"Catch her!" Marion was sprinting behind the mare.

Amy stretched out her arms. "Whoa, girl. Whoa!" Jasmine stumbled to a stop, blowing hard. Her bandages had unravelled and were trailing around her fetlocks.

"What's going on?" Amy exclaimed.

"I don't know," her mom puffed. "I was in Jake's stall and

heard hooves, and the next thing I knew, Jasmine was racing down the aisle."

"Oh, no," Amy groaned. She knew the concussion from the concrete would exacerbate the mare's condition.

Jasmine was trembling from cold and shock. Amy did her best to soothe her while Marion bent down to pull off the dirty bandages. "Let's get her back inside," she said the moment the bandages were free.

Amy clicked to the mare and led her back to her stall. "We're going to need to get the hose on those legs and then treat her all over again," Marion said. "I'll go heat the water for the wraps."

Amy put her hand under Jasmine's mane and moved her fingers in circles against the mare's damp coat. "Mom?" she questioned.

"Yes?" Marion asked, looking over her shoulder as she left the stall.

"Do you think Lou saw anything? You know, just now?"

"I don't think so," Marion said uncertainly. "I haven't seen her since lunch."

Marion's gaze lingered on Amy, and then she rushed down the aisle, leaving her with Jasmine. Amy was relieved that her sister had missed the commotion. She knew that Lou had been tentative around horses since their father's accident, and she didn't want to contribute to Lou's apprehension. The incident with Sundance had been bad enough; Amy didn't want her sister to think that every day revolved around some equine crisis.

"You'll be OK," she murmured to Jasmine. "We're going to take care of you, I promise." Amy reached down to feel the warm swelling around the mare's fetlocks and wondered how she had managed to get loose. Amy thought about how quiet Jasmine had seemed when she and Lou had checked on her, and an image of her sister fiddling with the door latch suddenly came to mind. She knew Lou would never have meant to let the pony out, but Amy thought it was likely that she had accidentally left the bolt for the door undone.

"Looks like I arrived just in time!" Scott's voice broke into Amy's thoughts. "Marion called and asked me to drop by. I gather Princess Jasmine has had an eventful day." He raised his eyebrows as he came into the stall, then crouched down and ran his hands over the mare's legs.

Amy could only nod.

"So, are you still coming to Matt's party tonight?" Scott's upbeat tone contrasted with the concern on his face as he examined Jasmine.

"Oh, yes." Amy had forgotten all about the party at Matt's house, and with everything that had been going on, it had slipped her mind that her mom had asked her to invite Lou along as well.

"Is everything OK?" There was the sound of footsteps in the aisle, and Lou's blonde head appeared over the door. "Mom said that the pony got out."

"Yes, she did," Amy said, still intently watching Scott.

Lou frowned. "Didn't you shut the door when you put her in this morning?"

"Yes, I did," Amy replied defensively, looking her sister in the eye. "But that doesn't do any good if someone comes along and loosens the bolt." The words rushed out of Amy's mouth before she could stop herself. Just moments earlier, Amy had wanted to keep a distance between Lou and all of the recent events. She thought if they could downplay the various horse crises, Lou would be more likely to get the most out of her time at Heartland. But Amy was no longer interested in protecting her sister, not when Lou's carelessness put the horse's welfare in danger.

An awkward silence filled the stall, and Lou's eyes widened as she registered Amy's accusation. "Will she be OK?" she said finally, directing her question to Scott.

"She'll be fine," the vet replied, his voice muffled. "As long as you spray cold water on her legs, you'll bring the swelling down soon enough," he told Amy, standing up. "I've got some gel packs in the Jeep that you can use on her, too."

"That's great, then," said Lou, before Amy could reply. "Everything's fine now."

Amy caught her breath in disbelief. She couldn't believe that Lou so easily dismissed the setback. There was no way to know how many weeks Jasmine's escape might have added to her recovery. Amy had a hard time believing Lou had ever spent time around a stable. She had little interest in Heartland's work, and she seemed to have forgotten how to shut a stable door!

Scott had been watching Amy's expression, and he turned quickly to Lou. "I don't know if Amy had mentioned it, but we're having a party at my house tonight. It would be great to see you."

Lou smiled warmly. "I'd love to come," she told him. "I'm not sure if I've got anything to wear, though."

"Oh, it's going to be casual," Scott told her, picking up his bag and shooting Amy a sympathetic glance as he let himself out of the stalls. "Are you headed in, Lou? If so, I'll go with you."

As Amy watched them make their way towards the house, she suddenly felt worn out. She bent down and rested her cheek against Jasmine's broad forehead. She didn't think it was possible that they'd rescued the little mare from the auction just hours earlier. Even though it was the best thing that could have happened for Jasmine, her arrival had made things even more strained between Amy and Lou. Perhaps the Trewins' party, an event far removed from the horse realm, was just what they needed to bring back some festive spirit and a real sense of family.

Chapter Eight

Amy looked down at the surface of her dressing table, which was littered with various compacts and kinds of make-up. "Lip gloss, lip gloss," she muttered to herself. She finally spotted it half-hidden under her hairbrush and pulled out the slim tube so she could roll on a layer over her light pink lipstick. She pressed her lips together and smiled at her reflection. It was nice to have an excuse to put on make-up. There was no point putting it on for the yard – it would get covered in mud and hay dust before she'd crossed the concrete, not to mention the fact that there was no one to see it. Other than Ty, of course, and he didn't count.

The sound of a car horn outside made her spin around to grab her bag from the bed. Lou was driving them both to the party in Marion's car. Amy's mom had originally intended to drop Amy off and pick her up again at midnight, but she had been very pleased when Lou had taken over chauffeur duty. It meant Marion would be able to keep a closer eye on Jasmine.

Amy picked up the pink cashmere stole that Lou had loaned her for the evening and felt a thrill of satisfaction with how well it set off the pink and black floral print of her skirt. She scooped up her flats and decided to put them on once she reached the bottom of the stairs so she wouldn't slip on the slick, unworn soles. The horn sounded again. "OK, I'm coming already," she called, switching off the light and running down the stairs.

Ty was in the kitchen washing his hands at the sink.

"I'm late," Amy announced breathlessly, strapping on her shoes.

"Your mom is still with Jasmine," Ty said without turning around. "She asked me to remind you to be home by twelve."

"You look gorgeous, sweetheart," said Jack, lowering his paper and peering at Amy over his reading glasses. "Are you sure you're going to be warm enough?"

"Grandpa! Like I care about being warm when I'm going to a party!" Amy laughed.

"Whoa!" Ty glanced over his shoulder and then turned fully around. "I would have bet that you couldn't do it, but you cleaned up in record time. And you look pretty good, too."

"Gee, thanks. You're dripping on the floor." Amy pointed to his hands, which were still covered in soap suds, and laughed. But for once Ty didn't have a fast comeback. He just wiped his hands on a dish towel and then lifted his eyes to meet hers.

Amy felt her cheeks turn scarlet, and she went to give her grandpa a hurried kiss. "See you later," she called, pulling open the door. She tried to ignore the cold draught that sent goose bumps racing over her skin.

"Midnight," Jack reminded her as she shut the door and picked her way towards the car, pulling the woollen stole tighter around her shoulders.

"You look nice," said Lou, releasing the brake.

"You, too," Amy smiled. Lou was wearing a chic blue silk dress that fell to just above her knees.

Amy wasn't sure what else to say. They hadn't talked about the afternoon's incident yet, but Amy wasn't sure she should bring it up right before the party.

"So, who's going to be there tonight?" Lou asked.

Amy noticed that her sister's voice was lighthearted and decided it was best to put their differences behind them and concentrate on having fun. "Scott, who you met earlier," Amy began. "His brother, Matt, and Soraya, and a whole bunch of guys from school. Mr and Mrs Trewin usually disappear into the den and leave us to have a suitably mature gathering on our own," Amy said in a voice of mock sophistication.

"I didn't realize that it was a high school party," Lou said after a pause.

"Well, it's not, exactly. Scott's in his twenties, and some of his friends will be there, too."

"OK, you'll have to give me directions from here," Lou said as she reached the end of the drive.

Amy told her which way to go, and they drove carefully along the dark roads until they arrived at the Trewins'. "I'll park on the street," Lou said, after noticing that the driveway had only two spaces left. "I don't want someone to come and block me in."

"Sure." Amy waited impatiently for her sister to manoeuvre into a space further up the street. The moment Lou pulled the keys out of the ignition, Amy bounded out of the car. "Do you want me to introduce you to everyone?" she asked as they made their way up the steps to the front door. She walked across the grand, white-pillared porch and rang the doorbell.

"I'll be fine." Lou waved her hand. "We do stuff like this all the time back home."

Amy was sure that her sister didn't mean to sound patronizing, but the words still irritated her. Maybe it was the casual way she referred to "we", obviously meaning her and Carl, or "home" meaning New York rather than Virginia. At least she hadn't meant England when she said "home" this time.

Fine, Amy thought as Matt pulled the door open, his face expectant and happy, *I'll leave you to do your own introductions and make your own friends.*

"Great, you're here!" Matt grinned. He took their wraps and led them into the living room, where the furniture had been covered with red throws and pushed back against the walls. Multicoloured Christmas lights were strung across the ceiling, and dance music was pulsing so loudly that Amy felt it throb through her as soon as she walked into the room. A large glitter ball hung above their heads, throwing back a kaleidoscope of lights as it spun in a slow circle.

"This is great!" she shouted at Matt, who squeezed her hand in response.

"Drink?" he offered, letting go of Amy's hand.

"I'll have some of the fruit punch," she said, pointing at the big silver bowl set out on the sideboard.

"White wine for me, please," Lou said.

"I'll get that." Scott looked over from where he had been chatting with a pretty brunette. Amy recalled Matt telling her that Scott was dating someone from his practice. "Victoria, I'd like you to meet Amy and her sister, Lou, who's home for the holidays from New York," Scott introduced his companion. "Victoria works with me," he added as Amy and Lou smiled politely.

"Come on." Matt pulled at Amy's sleeve. "Let's get you that drink. You look terrific, by the way."

"Thanks. You look good, too," Amy said, noticing that Matt was not in his usual uniform of jeans and an athletic T-shirt. Instead he had on black slacks and a tailored button-down shirt left untucked. Leaving Lou to chat with Scott and Victoria, she followed Matt through the crowded room to the dining room table. The music had changed to a slow song, and people were already starting to pair up.

She held out a glass and Matt ladled in the dark red punch.

"Mmm, this is really good," Amy said, sipping at the spicy liquid. "What's in it?"

"You'd have to ask my mom," Matt confessed.

Amy started to survey the room when she felt a tap on her shoulder. It was Soraya.

"You're here!" Soraya's eyes sparkled. "Isn't this a great party? Finish your drink and come dance!"

Amy laughed and quickly drained her glass. Soraya grabbed her hand and Amy noticed the hint of disappointment on Matt's face. She reached for his hand and tugged him along with them. "Come on, it's your party!" she told him. "You can't just stand on the sidelines."

Amy couldn't remember the last time she had been to such

a great party. She spent the next couple of hours dancing in a whirl of energy, stopping only to refill her glass. She noticed Lou talking to some of Scott's friends in the kitchen when she went for more ice. She was about to go over to make sure her sister was having a good time when her classmates Ellen and Robyn pulled her aside to fill her in on the latest news on several ongoing relationship sagas. Ellen and Robyn took it upon themselves to keep Amy's entire class informed on the gossip front. By the time she'd finished chatting with them, Lou had vanished.

"I need to go to the bathroom," Soraya spoke into her ear as Amy rejoined her and Matt on the dance floor.

"Me, too," Amy said. Promising Matt they wouldn't be long, the girls headed out into the hall and almost bumped into Lou, who was pulling her wrap from the bottom of the coat pile.

"I was just about to find you," she said to Amy.

"What?" Amy checked the time. "But it's only eleven!"

"Well, if you hadn't noticed, Scott and his friends disappeared half an hour ago to a club in town." Lou spoke with a sharp edge to her voice.

"You could have gone with them," Amy said.

"Yes, I could have, but then I wouldn't have been here to give you a ride home," Lou replied shortly.

"But there's still another hour before I have to go home!" Amy protested.

"Yes, and I'm ready to go now," Lou said. "So are you coming?"

"No," Amy said stubbornly. "I'll get a cab."

Lou raised her eyebrows. "Is Mom going to be comfortable with that?"

"She'll be fine," Amy told her, knowing full well that Marion wasn't happy with her taking cabs this late. "So you can go and I'll see you later."

Without giving Lou a chance to say anything else, she headed up the stairs to the bathroom, closely followed by Soraya. When they came back down, Lou had gone.

Amy pushed away the nagging worry that her mom was going to be very unimpressed with the change of plans. Her mom wouldn't be in favour of her taking a cab alone during the day, let alone late on an icy night. She was determined to get as much as she could out of her last hour at the party. She smiled at Matt, who was holding out plates for them. "Mom finally unveiled the refreshments," he explained. "She made a big deal about it – she's been baking for a week. If you're lucky, there might be some fruitcake left."

Amy and Soraya rushed past Matt and headed for the back room. There, a snowy white tablecloth was covered with tempting dishes that all still had plenty left on them. Amy piled her plate with cheese, crackers, grapes and half a dozen different desserts, and then squeezed on to a sofa with Matt on one side and Soraya on the other. They chatted as they ate, and then, when Amy's favourite song came on, she dumped her plate on the table beside the sofa and jumped up to dance.

The next time she looked at her watch she couldn't believe

how much time had gone by. It was a quarter to one in the morning!

Amy excused herself and tried to find a phone to call a cab. When she finally got through, the dispatcher said that there wouldn't be any cars for at least an hour.

"Are you sure?" Amy asked.

"I'm positive," he replied in a tired, gruff voice.

Amy hung up the phone and checked her watch again. It was just after one. She picked up the phone to call her mom, suspecting it was best to cut her losses, but then she replaced the receiver. The last thing she wanted was to wake up Marion. Besides, she was already an hour late, so if she was going to be in trouble anyway, she'd be better off not disturbing her mother's beauty sleep.

Amy made her way downstairs and searched the first floor. About half of their classmates were still there, but the party was showing signs of winding down, with one indistinguishable ballad after another playing as a few couples swayed in the middle of the room.

Matt appeared at her shoulder. "Do you want to dance this one with me?"

Amy stared at him, stricken. "Matt, I can't, I'm sorry. I promised my mom that I'd be home at twelve, and there aren't any available cabs."

"Of course there aren't," Matt replied. "It's the holidays and this is Virginia. It's not like there's a fleet of empty yellow taxis at every corner."

Soraya overheard them and pulled away from her dance

partner, who looked half asleep anyway. "Hey, no worries," she reassured Amy. "My dad's picking me up in five minutes. We can drop you off."

"Thanks, I'll just go grab my wrap," Amy said gratefully. Soraya's dad took closer to twenty minutes to show up. Amy and Matt sat on the sofa and watched as Soraya played musical dance partners for the remainder of the playlist.

Amy was quiet once they got in the car. The night had whirled by in a flash of sound and colour, but now time seemed to drag. She couldn't help wondering what kind of reception would be waiting for her when she finally got home.

The kitchen lights were still on when Mr Martin dropped her off by the house. Amy pressed down the door handle as quietly as she could and tiptoed into the house. Her heart sank when she saw Marion dozing in the corner chair. She had her old blue bathrobe around her, and one of the veterinary journals Scott had loaned her was open on her lap.

Amy hesitated, torn between going straight up to bed and facing her mom in the morning or getting the confrontation out of the way now.

Marion solved Amy's dilemma. Opening her eyes, she blinked a few times, looked straight at Amy and then at her watch. Amy waited awkwardly as she flipped the journal shut and stood up.

"Look, before you start, I'm really sorry. I just didn't notice the time, OK?" she blurted out.

Marion's blue eyes narrowed. "What you mean is, you didn't

care about the time." She spoke in the ominously calm voice that Amy recognized from the auction.

Amy felt stung by the unfairness of her mother's accusation. "That's not true! I did care!"

"Your sister left you at eleven and told you that you only had an hour left. You can't expect me to believe that *three hours* slipped past without you realizing it," Marion snapped, slamming the journal down on the table.

Amy's temper flared. "That's right, my sister left me. If Lou had been willing to stay another forty-five minutes, we wouldn't be having this discussion. Your car would have pulled into the Heartland driveway as the clock struck twelve and your two happy daughters would have come in the door giggling and holding hands. Everything would have been great." Amy drew a deep breath. She heard how cruel and hard her own voice sounded – hardly like herself at all. "But that's not what happened. She left and when I tried to call a cab, they were all out! All Lou had to do was spend some time with me, but what she really wanted was to go into town, because a small-town house party isn't up to her city standards."

"Amy, I am not doing this with you now," Marion said. "I have to be up to see to the horses in four hours." Her tone was icy. "I never thought of you as selfish, but I've seen a side of you tonight that I don't like very much."

"Well, I don't like the fact that you are automatically taking Lou's side." Amy was hardly aware of what she was saying. "You're both jealous that I actually managed to have a good time tonight. It's not like I get the chance that often!" She took a deep breath. "You didn't have to wait up for me. No one asked you to. You could have gone to bed, and it wouldn't have mattered that I was late. I mean, it's the holidays. What's the big deal?"

Marion raised her voice. "If you can't figure out what the big deal is, then you should do some serious thinking. Not everything revolves around you, you know. Do you remember what we were talking about earlier? How it should be give and take when you work with horses? Well, it's no different in your relationships with people. And I'd like to see more giving and less taking from you, young lady. Maybe then you'd prove you're grown up enough that I don't have to wait up for you!"

Amy's mouth dropped open. "Fine," she said finally.

"I would have thought you'd have learned better working at Heartland." Marion said it more softly, but her voice was just as intense.

"Yeah," Amy scoffed. "Of course it all comes down to Heartland. Don't worry, I won't forget where your priorities are. Of all your children, you love it the best."

Without waiting for her mom's response, she ran from the kitchen. She didn't stop until she had flung herself on to her bed with her arms over her head, feeling hot tears running down her cheeks. She cried until the pain was gone, and she cried some more. And then she slept.

Chapter Nine

When Amy woke up, she had the feeling that something was missing, but she didn't know what. She groaned as the memory of the fight with her mom forced itself back into her head, slowly at first and then in a rush. She picked up her alarm clock, and when she saw that it was only seven o'clock, thought for a moment about trying to go back to sleep. But she knew she wouldn't be able to doze off. She was destined to lie there turning the argument over and over in her head until she actually confronted her mom and committed herself to apologizing.

It was only as she was pulling on a thick pair of socks that Amy remembered it was Christmas Eve. She let out a hollow laugh. She couldn't remember a time when it had felt less like Christmas. She stood up and had to sit back down on the bed with a thump. Her head was pounding like a jackhammer, and she wondered if her mom had experienced just as restless a night.

Amy could hear the sound of her grandpa whistling carols when she walked downstairs, and she tried hard to conjure up a little festive spirit. She pushed open the door to the kitchen and was hit by a strong scent of orange peel.

"Morning!" Jack called cheerfully.

His merry greeting convinced Amy that her mother had kept

their discussion between just the two of them. Amy headed over to the kitchen counter to give Grandpa a kiss and to investigate the incredible smell. She had almost forgotten that her grandpa made his special muffins every Christmas Eve by soaking orange peel and raisins in rum.

"What's that gorgeous aroma?" Lou followed Amy into the kitchen and sniffed the air appreciatively. Her blonde hair was pulled back with barrettes and her cheeks were a rosy pink. She looked the happiest she had been since arriving, which made Amy feel even worse.

"I'm just going to find Mom," Amy said, walking straight through the kitchen to the back door and pulling on her coat. She didn't want Lou to start asking her about how she had got home last night.

"Don't you want a muffin? The first batch will be out in five minutes," Jack called after her.

"I'll be back soon, thanks," Amy said, before escaping out into the crisp early morning air.

She found Marion in the schooling ring riding Pegasus. Amy leaned on the gate and watched them perform a shoulder-in down one side of the ring. In spite of his age and the accident, the big grey Thoroughbred had a wonderful floating action. His tail was kinked and his head arched as he concentrated on the directives Marion was giving. Amy watched her mom sit perfectly still, riding in perfect sympathy with the beautiful grey horse. At the far end, Marion turned up the centre line and halted Pegasus before reining back. He performed the movement calmly before halting again, his hooves perfectly square. As Marion reached down and patted Pegasus's neck, Amy clapped.

Marion looked up with a startled expression on her face. She had clearly been concentrating so hard that she hadn't noticed Amy watching. She pushed Pegasus into a trot and slid off him once he had reached the gate.

"Hey, Pegasus," Amy said, reaching up to scratch his forehead. Now that her mom was in front of her she felt tongue-tied and flustered. She sneaked a look at Marion and noticed dark rings around her eyes. Amy's heart clenched with guilt and sadness. "I'm really sorry, Mom," she burst out. "I can't believe I said all that stuff last night. I promise I didn't stay out late on purpose. I was just having so much fun, and then it wasn't as easy to get home as I thought it would be."

Marion slipped her arm through the reins and reached forward to wrap her arms around Amy. "I said some pretty awful things, too. It's because I was tired and worried about you. If you want to talk about it, we can. I'm sure it hasn't been that easy on you having Lou here and still trying to keep up with everything happening with Heartland."

"It's not so bad," Amy said.

"Well, I know I'm having a hard time," Marion confided. "I want Lou to have a real holiday. I mean, we see her so seldom. But it's hard to do all the things that make this time of year special when you spend half the day knee-deep in manure."

Amy gazed up at her mom, who was looking towards the farmhouse. "Grandpa made his muffins," she offered. "I bet they're about to come out of the oven right now."

"Well, that sounds like a holiday tradition just waiting for us," Marion said, giving Amy a squeeze before letting her go. She slid the reins off her arm and spoke more briskly. "No doubt he's brewing some homemade hot chocolate, too. Let's get Pegasus settled and head inside. After all, it's Christmas!"

"Yes, it is," Amy said happily.

The first thing Amy noticed when they walked into the kitchen was a black suitcase and matching carry-on pushed up against the wall.

"What's going on?" she asked Lou, who was just hanging up the phone.

Lou's blue eyes, so like their mom's, were shining. "I know this might come as a bit of a shock," she said, "but I've decided to cut the holiday a little short."

"How short?" Amy demanded bluntly.

Lou looked from her to their mom. "I've booked a flight for this afternoon."

Amy shook her head in confusion. "What? Why? You promised to stay with us for Christmas." Her mind was in a whirl. "I cleaned up your room!"

Marion walked over to the sink and got a glass from the drying rack. She filled it with water and took a few sips before pouring out the rest and turning to face Lou. Her face was pale, but she managed a tight-lipped smile. "Well," she said, her voice sounding a little forced, "the only thing that's important to us is that you're happy and spending the season with who you want to be with."

Lou hesitated. "Carl called last night and said he was missing me," she explained. "He said he'd pay for my ticket if I could get a flight home in time to spend Christmas with him."

Digging her nails into her palms, Amy thought that it was one of the most selfish things she had ever heard. It was exactly what she would have expected of Carl, who obviously didn't understand how much Lou's family might want to spend the holiday with her, given they saw her only twice a year.

"He really wants to spend Christmas with me," Lou said, her face lit up with happiness as she unwittingly echoed Amy's thoughts.

"So do we," Amy said, crossing her arms.

Lou looked pleadingly at Amy and held out her hand. "I'm so sorry if you're disappointed."

If? Amy thought of all the family holiday traditions they hadn't shared. They hadn't decorated the tree, played board games, or drunk eggnog, not to mention opened presents or eaten Christmas dinner.

"Well, it's worked out perfectly, because we've had a wonderful time together, and now you can have a great time with Carl, too. So we've all been able to share you this Christmas," Marion said brightly.

"Thanks, Mom," Lou said, flashing her a smile.

Can't you see how disappointed she is? Amy thought, clenching her fists even tighter.

"I was going to get a taxi, but Grandpa offered to drop me off at the airport. He's just getting changed," Lou added.

"No, he's not. He's all ready to go." Jack walked into the

kitchen wearing a clean checked shirt. "I managed to get flour all over me making those muffins, despite my apron." He winked at Amy. "And you know what I got to thinking upstairs? Maybe Lou's young man is going to pop the question this Christmas and that's why he's in such a rush to get her home!"

"Grandpa," Lou protested. "I'm sure he's not going to do any such thing." But her cheeks were flushed, and Amy could see that it had crossed her sister's mind at least once that a proposal might be in the cards.

"I'm just going to go check on Jasmine," Amy muttered, feeling desperate to escape and pull her thoughts together. "I'll be back in a couple of minutes." The last thing she wanted was a fight with Lou just before she left. But if she stayed any longer she knew that she would say something harsh to her sister about deserting them and heading back to the city. They hadn't even had time to catch up.

She got as far as the bench inside the barn doors and sank down on to it with her hands wrapped around her knees. She felt like nothing was going right. The visit with Lou hadn't been anything like what she had planned, she'd had a major fight with her mom that had spoiled her big night out, and she still felt like she was failing with Sundance, whatever she did – and she didn't even have the nerve to talk to her mom about it. The show was less than two days away, and Amy had no idea how to break it to Marion that the pony wasn't ready, especially now that Lou was going home early.

"Hey, sweetheart." Jack's voice broke into her thoughts as he came into the barn after her. "You know, I'm disappointed that

Lou's leaving us, too. But it's not going to spoil our Christmas, I promise. The three of us will still have a great time."

Amy looked up at him and managed a smile.

"That's better," said Jack, holding out his hands to her. "We only have a few minutes left with Lou, so when we go back to the house, we should be as cheerful as possible, because we don't know when the four of us will be together again. We need to make every moment count."

Amy thought it would be much easier to make every moment count if Lou wouldn't leave as soon as she came, but she knew Grandpa was right. They should salvage what they could of their family time.

When they reached the house, Lou was already loading her bags into Jack's car. "I'm all set," she smiled. She held out her arms to Amy.

"I'll miss you," Amy said, knowing that she would. But in a way, she was going to miss the holiday they could have had most of all.

"Me, too," said Lou, releasing her to hug Marion. "Thanks for a lovely time, Mom."

"Call us when you get in," Marion said, blinking quickly.

"I will," Lou promised, getting into the car alongside Jack. She wound down the window and waved until the car disappeared down the drive. Amy felt a cold, heavy sadness creep over her as she realized that she didn't know when she would see Lou again.

"Right," Marion said briskly. "I'm going to go hose down Jasmine's legs again and give her some more of the arnica." She ran her hand through her tangled blonde hair. "Can you make a start on filling the hay nets for tonight, dear? It's Ty's day off and I'm already way behind on everything that needs to be done."

"OK," Amy said, tilting her head as she heard the distant ringing of the phone. "I'll just go answer that first."

"Don't call me unless it's urgent," Marion added as she strode off in the direction of the barn, and Amy realized that her mom was acting like Lou was always supposed to leave today. She raced for the phone and snatched up the receiver. It was Soraya, who explained that she had just got out of bed after sleeping in.

"Did you get into trouble with your mom?" she asked anxiously.

"Oh, there was major strife last night, but it's OK now," Amy told her. The shock of Lou's leaving had overshadowed her fight with Marion.

"I'm going into town to get my mom's Christmas present," Soraya went on. "I know it's Christmas Eve and the mall will be really busy, but it could be fun. Do you want to come?"

Amy thought for a moment. She had got all of her presents the last time she was in town and she didn't really have an excuse to go, but part of her longed to get away.

"We could maybe catch a movie – the classic version of *A Christmas Carol* is playing at the Drexel," Soraya added.

Amy was very tempted. It might as well be the middle of February at Heartland for the lack of festivities going on. It felt like Lou had packed up all the Christmas decorations and holiday cheer and taken them with her. "Ty!" she exclaimed suddenly.

"Huh?"

"I haven't bought Ty anything for Christmas yet, so I'll have to come into town," Amy told her, feeling a flood of relief at having found an excuse to escape for a while. She made arrangements to meet up with Soraya and then rushed out to the feed room to prepare the evening feeds as fast as possible.

She tied all of the hay nets up in the empty stalls before fetching the extra two she had filled for Sundance and Jasmine, who weren't able to be turned out.

"How's she doing?" she asked her mom as she let herself into Jasmine's stall.

"Her legs are still swollen from her sprint across the yard yesterday." Marion didn't look up from bandaging Jasmine's legs. There was a strong aroma filling the stable.

"Lavender?" Amy asked, wrinkling her nose.

Marion nodded. "To keep her relaxed."

Amy smoothed her hand down Jasmine's satiny shoulder and was pleased at the way the black mare turned her head to give her a friendly nudge. She picked up the hay net and tied it to the ring at the back of the stall.

"I'm just going to give Sundance his afternoon hay net," she said to her mom.

The buckskin gelding was resting in the far corner of his stall, and Amy didn't bother trying to approach him. She tied his hay net and retreated, bolting the door firmly behind her. Her mom joined her and leaned on the door to look at Sundance, who was watching them with his ears pricked.

"Here, Sunny," Marion coaxed, holding out a sliced carrot.

Sundance walked towards them, stopping short of the door. He eyed the carrot suspiciously before reaching out and taking it off her palm. He came closer, looking for more carrot, and Marion gave him the last slice. "It's a shame that Lou won't be around to see you at the show," she said after a pause.

Amy felt herself freeze inside and couldn't think what to say in reply.

"You must be disappointed, too," Marion went on, without looking at Amy. She fiddled with a splinter on the door. "But I have to say that I think we made the mistake of expecting Lou to fit into our routine while she was here, instead of respecting that she has a completely different lifestyle." Her voice was thoughtful. "Just because it's different, it doesn't make it wrong. She's very successful in the city and very happy, too. That's all I want for both of you."

At that moment, Sundance kicked the door in temper at there being no more carrots. "Oh, cut it out!" Amy snapped.

Marion blinked and pushed a strand of hair out of her eyes. "Amy?" she asked softly. "Is something else wrong?"

Her mom's question was sincere, and Amy felt guilty for having put off their conversation about Sundance for so long. Still, she doubted that this was the right time. But as she looked up at Marion, she suddenly knew that she owed it to her mom to tell her the truth, no matter how difficult it might be. Just because Lou had changed her plans unexpectedly didn't mean their mom wouldn't want to be there for Amy. She took a deep breath. "I don't really want to compete at the show."

Marion looked puzzled. "But why?"

Amy hesitated, keeping her eyes fixed on the buckskin gelding, who was rubbing his head against the top of the door.

"Well?" Marion prompted.

"We're just not ready. Every time I've got on him recently, he's been a total nightmare," Amy said in a rush.

Marion narrowed her eyes. "What does he do?"

"He denies the bit, pulls, and bulges. Sometimes he's good on the flat, but then he'll freak out at the sight of a jump and take off. It's like he's determined to fight me, no matter what I do, but I can't figure out why," Amy confessed.

"How long has it been?"

"Well, it started slowly at first — he just seemed high-spirited. I could handle that — but lately he's been out of control. Yesterday, he bolted straight for the gate. He was at a full gallop and only skidded to a stop a stride away." She looked up into her mom's concerned gaze.

Marion drummed her fingers on the door. "You know, it sounds to me like you've lost faith in each other."

Sundance chose that moment to let out a long sigh, as if he were agreeing with her. Amy gave a small nod. "I do feel like we've lost any connection there was between us in the summer," she admitted. "But I can't think of anything that's happened to make him change."

"There's always the cooler weather. He no doubt has more energy, but it's more than that." Marion pushed her fingers though her hair while she looked first at Sundance and then back to Amy. A frown creased her forehead and she seemed to be weighing her words. "Well, have you thought about joining up with him?" she said at last. "I know you haven't tried it before, but it's the only thing I can think of that might help the two of you get back the bond you had before. I can put some remedies into his feed to try and calm him, but it's only by joining up that you will gain his complete trust."

Amy appreciated her mom's advice, but when she looked at Sundance, he was tugging viciously at his net and tossing his head as he ate, like he even had something against his hay. Amy knew deep down that she had lost all her will to try and work with the gelding. She glanced back at Marion's hopeful expression and felt her heart deflate as she tried to find the words to refuse her mom's offer. She just felt she had done all she could for Sundance, and that it would be better if he were sold so she could concentrate on riding the other horses at Heartland. She opened her mouth to give Marion a flat refusal, but faltered when she saw her mom's intense gaze. "Well, I guess that could work," Amy said slowly. "But what if he doesn't respond? He doesn't even lunge well any more."

"Don't worry, I'll take you through it," Marion promised. "You don't have to do it on your own."

Amy knew that she didn't want to join up with Sundance, but she wasn't prepared to tell her mom that right now and add to her already long list of recent disappointments. She picked at a piece of dirt trapped under her fingernail, searching for a change of subject. "Soraya called earlier," she said. "She wants me to meet her in town. I still need to get Ty's present, so is it OK if I go? I've done all of the hay nets," she added, looking up.

A look of disappointment flashed across Marion's face. "You

can go in with me on Ty's gift," she offered.

"Mom," Amy droned, recognizing her mother's attempt to keep her from going. "Ty's my friend, too. I want to get him something from me."

Marion gave her a long look. "Don't give up on Sundance," she said quietly.

"I'm not!" Amy forced herself to sound positive. "It's just that I've got shopping to do, but I promise I'll think about the join-up. Thanks for this, Mom," she added, reaching up to kiss her cheek before racing down the aisle.

"Amy!" Marion's voice stopped her just as she was about to push open the barn door.

"Yes?"

"Have you exercised Sundance today?"

"Yes," Amy called back and hurried from the barn, trying to ignore the nagging voice in her head that said, *No, you haven't.*

But she knew that if she had admitted that, her mom might have insisted she work with him instead of going shopping. *I can always turn him out into the ring when I get back,* she thought. *It's so cold, he won't want to be out for long anyway.*

When Amy finally arrived back home, it was dark. She waved goodbye to Soraya and Mrs Martin, who had given her a ride, and turned to go into the house, invigorated by her busy afternoon. Every store had been playing Christmas songs, and everywhere Amy had looked there had been Santas and elves and snowmen and reindeer, all surrounded with tinsel, glitter and snow. Sure, the mall had been busier than a week of Saturdays rolled into one, but everyone seemed to be in a great mood as they bustled from one shop to another, and Amy felt as if she and Soraya hadn't stopped laughing once.

Humming a carol, she pushed open the kitchen door and smiled at Lou's holly wreath, which suddenly seemed like a really nice idea. But when she walked into the kitchen, she was struck by how unfestive the farmhouse looked. There wasn't even a garland on the mantelpiece, and the latest installment of cards that had come in the mail were still in a stack on the table rather than hanging over the string that Lou had pinned along one rafter.

Amy's mom and grandpa were eating sandwiches at the table. "You're later than I expected," said Marion, giving her a tired smile.

"We decided to catch a movie," Amy said awkwardly.

"Was it any good?" asked Jack, pushing a plate across the table to her.

"Yes, thanks," said Amy, feeling even more uncomfortable. She could sense an underlying tension, even though Marion and Jack hadn't reprimanded her for being out the entire afternoon.

"Why don't I put together something nice for dinner?" she said, putting down her bag. She wanted to make up for being out so long.

"We don't have any food," Marion said shortly. "The only thing in the freezer is lamb, which we have to save for tomorrow."

"Lamb?" Amy echoed. "But it's Christmas Day! Why aren't we having turkey?"

"I'm afraid our wires got crossed," Jack explained apologetically. "Lou said that she'd get the groceries. She probably forgot all about it when she changed her plans."

Amy tried to preserve her good mood. "Well, sandwiches are fine by me. So is lamb. I'm just going to wrap my present for Ty, and then we can get started trimming the tree?" She glanced anxiously at her grandfather. "If you've had time to get one, that is."

Jack smiled at her. "I most certainly did. I cut one down when I came back from dropping Lou off at the airport. It's smaller than usual because I didn't have time to wrestle a big one, but at least we have something to decorate, which is the main thing."

"Sundance needs his evening hay net," Marion interrupted. She dropped her head into her hands and began to massage her temples, and Amy thought that she looked more tired than ever. "I fed all of the others, but he still had half a net left from earlier. He should have finished it by now."

"I'll take care of it," Amy told her. "It won't take me more than a couple of minutes."

She pulled her jacket closer to her neck as she walked out to the barn. The sky was completely clear, silvered with a full moon and a million twinkling stars. *It's not too late to turn Christmas around,* Amy thought, determined not to feel resentful of Lou for leaving them high and dry. As soon as she got back to the house, she would find something more festive to eat while they decorated. She would wrap the gloves that she had bought for Ty and put them under the tree along with all the other gifts, and maybe they could even play some Christmas carols.

Humming, she collected Sundance's hay net from the feed room and clicked on the light inside the barn. Usually the gelding would be hanging his head out of the door, impatient for his evening feed, but there was no sign of him this time. Some of the other horses looked out at the sound of her footsteps.

"Hey, Spice." Amy smiled as the roan horse raised his head and nickered to her. She stopped at the next stall down and peered in. Sundance was lying down and didn't even bother looking up.

"Sundance! Come on, boy. I've got your evening hay net, last meal of the day," Amy told him. She noticed that the net she had put in his stall earlier was still only half eaten. A faint thread of worry stirred inside her, like a wisp of hay lifted by the breeze.

"Sundance! Get up, boy," she said again. She couldn't figure out why he was lying down. He should be bursting with energy, since she hadn't been back in time to turn him out. The tremor of worry settled in her gut and grew, tinged with guilt.

Amy dropped the hay net and opened the door. She stopped a few feet short of Sundance and hesitated before bending down and taking hold of his halter. "Up," she said, pulling.

The gelding let out a low groan and slowly scrambled to his feet. Amy let go of his halter. "That's better," she told him. "Now, how about some nice fresh hay?"

She fetched the net, but as she started to go back into the stall she stopped abruptly and her heart dropped like a stone. Sundance was swinging his head around to nip at his stomach with his tail clamped close to his hindquarters.

It was one of the first things that horses did when they had colic.

"No, please, no," Amy whispered. Sundance swung his head around again, and Amy's heart jumped back to life and began to pound. Without waiting another second, she dropped the net and raced back down the aisle.

"Mom!" she shouted. "Mom, you have to come!"

Chapter Ten

Marion took one look at Sundance and shook her head. The buckskin gelding was lying down again. He had obviously rolled, because the bedding around him was flattened and bits of straw clung to his coat.

"We've got to get him up. We can't let him roll again. Who knows what harm he's already done," Marion declared. She hurried into the stall and crouched down by Sundance, grasping his halter. "Come on, boy, up," she said firmly, just as Amy had done moments before.

Jack joined them and looked at Sundance, his face creased with worry. "I'll phone Scott," he said, and without waiting for them to reply, he hurried away.

By now, Marion had Sundance on his feet. Even without a thermometer, Amy could see that he was running a temperature. His face and ears were dark with sweat. "Go get a cooler," Marion told her as she walked Sundance past. "I'm taking him out to the yard where there's more room."

With her heart thudding, Amy raced to the tack room and pulled down a cooler from one of the blanket rails. She knew that the wool blanket would draw the sweat off Sundance's body while protecting him from the cold temperature outside.

Marion was slowly walking Sundance around the yard. The buckskin's head was held low, and his ears flopped listlessly as he made slow progress across the concrete, sometimes flinching and then stumbling forward. Running from the barn, Amy thought the moonlight slanting across Marion's face gave her an ethereal, almost angelic quality. Marion's eyes were fixed on Sundance as she walked backward, urging him to keep with her, to keep strong.

"I've got the cooler," Amy said quietly.

"Hold him while I put it on," said her mom, handing Amy the lead rope and unbuckling the chest straps on Sundance's stable sheet.

Amy held the rope, noticing that there was not even a flicker in Sundance's eyes to show that he was aware of her standing there. She felt a sudden rush of longing for his usual strong-willed, bad-tempered personality and reached up her hand to rub his forehead. "Oh, Sundance, you poor boy," she whispered, feeling utterly useless.

Sundance curled his upper lip and swung his head around at his stomach as a spasm passed along his flank, which was taut like a drum.

Amy was amazed that she could actually see the tension in his body, the swell in his abdomen. "Hold him still," Marion said, as she began buckling up the cooler.

Amy held the pony's head against her chest, stroking his cheek while she murmured soothingly. Sundance pawed at the ground, scraping against the concrete with his iron shoe. The noise shattered the still of the night air.

"OK. Start walking him again," Marion ordered. "We need to keep him on the move to help unknot the muscles."

Amy nodded. She knew all about the dangers of colic. They needed to keep him walking as long as possible, and they couldn't let him eat or drink. Most important, they couldn't let him roll for fear he would twist his intestines, which would more than likely be fatal. Shuddering, she pulled at Sundance's rope, but the pony braced himself against her weight and tossed his head. Even in a weakened state, he was stronger than she.

"Come on, boy." Marion took hold of the other side of Sundance's halter and clicked him on. When the gelding began to clop his way around again, she said, "I can't understand what triggered the colic." She shot Amy a glance over Sundance's head. "I thought we had it beat. He's been in good shape and worked regularly. We haven't changed his grain or done anything that would hinder his digestion. Keeping him off the winter grass and adding the peppermint oil to his feed should have kept things stable."

Amy was quiet. A rush of guilt swept over her, telling her that she hadn't done her part. She had not been taking care of Sundance properly and working him regularly, but she pushed those thoughts away.

"Is there anything that you can think of, Amy, that might have made him sick?" It was as if her mom had read her mind. Amy shook her head and reached up to rub Sundance's ears. All she wanted to concentrate on was making him well again.

The kitchen door banged open and Jack came out holding two mugs of steaming coffee. "Scott is on his way," he told them. "Let me walk him while you drink these."

Amy was reluctant to let go of Sundance, but she knew

Grandpa would keep him on his feet and not allow him to roll. She uncurled her fingers, cold inside her thick wool gloves, and handed the lead rein to Jack.

His blue eyes were kind. "All right, dear," he said.

Amy cupped her hands around the mug and joined her mother, who was watching Sundance anxiously. "I just don't understand," she said under her breath.

It was no use. Amy knew she had kept enough from her mom already. "Could not riding him enough have anything to do with it?" she said quietly, her words dropping like stones into the still night air.

Marion lowered her mug. Her eyes were very serious. "What do you mean?"

Amy gazed at Sundance, plodding beside Jack with his head down. He looked so listless, totally unrecognizable from the feisty pony she knew so well. "Over the last couple of weeks, I haven't been riding him much," she admitted, feeling her stomach tighten. "You know how I told you that I've been having problems? Well, it was worse than I let on. He was so bad that I avoided riding him. And some days I gave up after a short workout."

"How long has he been in that stable?" Marion asked without raising her voice.

Amy licked her lips, feeling a defensive wave of protest rise in her. "I've only left him in two or three times! When I didn't ride, I turned him out into the schooling ring."

"And today?"

Amy shifted her feet awkwardly. "I didn't exercise him like I said. I'm sorry." Her voice wasn't much more than a whisper. "I . . . I lied."

Marion didn't answer, and the silence hung between them like bitter-tasting smoke.

"Are you angry?" Amy said finally.

Her mom looked straight at her, her eyes filled with a score of emotions that Amy couldn't name. "I should be angry with you, but I'm not. I'm just disappointed. If you didn't want responsibility for Sundance, then all you had to do was tell me and I would have taken care of him."

Her words turned to ice and stabbed Amy's heart. This was far, far worse than if her mom had yelled at her.

Without saying another word, Marion put her mug down on the doorstep and walked back to Sundance. Amy glanced at the bright lights of the kitchen, tempting her inside with warmth and shelter, and then she looked back at her mom and Jack walking on either side of Sundance. Without hesitating, she went over to her grandpa and said, "I'll take over now."

Jack nodded. "I'll go get the funnel," he said. "Some saline water might help ease the spasm in his gut. If we can get him to take it."

Amy took hold of Sundance's lead rope and felt a wave of alarm as the pony staggered back, his eyes rolling and flashing white with fear.

"Pull him forward! He wants to roll!" Marion urged, tugging at Sundance's halter.

"Walk on, boy!" Amy called, pulling against Sundance's heavy weight.

She felt almost giddy with relief when, with a low moan, Sundance gave in and stepped forward. Her heart was pounding and she was sick with guilt, even though she didn't fully understand how not exercising Sundance had given him colic. After they had completed another circle of the yard, she needed to know exactly what she had done wrong – what had made Sundance sick.

"Horses that are prone to colic always need extra care, like regular feeding and exercise," Marion told her. "But actually, I have a feeling the problem was in your turning him out in the schooling ring. If he's been eating the sand in there, even just sniffing it out of boredom, it can easily trigger colic. The granules can really irritate a horse's system, especially a horse that's already prone to digestive problems."

Amy bit her lip and gazed at the floor. There was no way around it. Given that information, Sundance's suffering was her fault.

She forced herself to look at her mom again. "I want to help," she said. "I know I've let Sundance down – and you, too – and I want to do whatever I can to make things right. I want to help make Sundance better."

Marion narrowed her eyes and nodded. "You can start by getting me some peppermint extract mixed with henbane. And some of the rock rose remedy to take away his fear of the pain. We should also get an aromatherapy oil to rub into his flanks. You'll have to check my notebooks to find out which one will help fight the pain and tightness the most."

"OK," said Amy, patting Sundance's damp neck before handing the lead rope to Marion.

"And Amy?" her mother said quietly.

Amy turned. "Yes?"

"There are no guarantees that Sundance will get better. If his colic gets worse, we might not be able to do enough for him." Marion's voice was strained. "You have to be ready for that."

Amy's stomach turned over. She looked at Sundance pawing at the ground and tossing his head. She knew her mom wasn't trying to be harsh, yet her words had been a warning. She whirled around and raced for the feed room.

Her fingers were trembling as she hunted through Marion's stores of remedies. When she picked up the peppermint, she knocked over a row of other bottles. She tried taking deep breaths to calm down as she set them quickly upright again.

She pulled her mother's aromatherapy notebook from the top drawer of the battered wooden cupboard. "C," she said out loud, running her finger down the index. Marion's bold handwriting under the heading of "colic" read:

PAIN RELIEF — to ease the pain of colic the blend of basil, elemi, grapefruit, lavender & rosemary oils reduces stress & relieves pain, helping the horse to become more cooperative for other treatments. (C15)

Amy left the book lying open on the cupboard and hunted through the aromatherapy bottles on the shelf for one labelled C15. As soon as she had found it and double-checked that the other remedies were in her pocket, she hurried back to the yard.

The pony had halted underneath one of the outdoor lights, and Marion was moving her fingers in small circles on Sundance's neck. Amy knew that she was using the T-touch massage technique to try to relax him.

"Hold out your hand," Marion said. Taking the bottle of rock rose, she squeezed several drops into Amy's outstretched palm. "Now let him lick it."

Amy held her hand below Sundance's nose. He ignored it, his head nodding slightly. He seemed to be standing as still as possible. "You need to be quick. We have to keep him walking," Marion said, sounding tense.

"Come on, Sunny," Amy begged, smoothing her other hand down his cheek. She put her hand in the corner of his mouth and he instinctively opened it.

After a moment he seemed to become aware of her hand, and he ran his tongue over her palm, licking off all of the rock rose.

"Good boy," Amy said. She held out her hand again to Marion, this time for the peppermint and henbane mixture. "And this will make him feel better?" she asked, without taking her eyes off Sundance, who obediently licked the liquid this time.

"Yes, it's a natural painkiller," Marion said.

Amy gasped as Sundance suddenly lunged at his stomach, his teeth bared. Marion pulled back his head. "No! Quick, Amy! We have to get him walking again."

Amy's heart thudded against her ribs. "He doesn't understand!" she gasped. "He doesn't know why he's in so much pain."

Sundance grunted and kicked at his stomach. Marion strained against the lead line. "Come on, boy. Walk!" she cried while Jack hurried over carrying a canister and a funnel.

"It took me ages to find the funnel," he told them breathlessly. "It was buried in the tack room. And there wasn't any saline, so I brought liquid paraffin instead."

"OK, Dad, let's get some in him quickly!" Marion urged, just as headlights swept into the yard.

Amy felt weak with relief at the sight of Scott's Jeep. The vet jumped out, grabbed his bag from the backseat, and then ran towards them. "I thought we'd seen the last of these attacks," he said, his expression grim.

"So did I," said Marion. "And I'm afraid it's a bad one."

Amy felt her heart lurch, and her feet stumbled against the concrete walk. Sundance threw up his head and tucked his quarters under him, trying to halt, but Amy tugged on the lead rope and he staggered forward again.

"He hasn't had all of the exercise that he's used to lately," Marion told him, "and he's been turned out into the schooling ring a few times, so there's a chance he might have eaten some sand."

"Well, that would do it," Scott responded immediately.

Amy felt a guilty relief, knowing that her mom had not outwardly blamed her. She guessed it wasn't important now, when the only thing that mattered was getting Sundance well again.

Scott had already put down his bag and had his stethoscope pressed against Sundance's flank. Amy reached out and gripped her mom's arm as the vet listened intently. Scott didn't say a word as he took Sundance's temperature, but he frowned when he saw the reading. "His temperature is much higher than I'd like," he said. "Since there's a chance that he's got sand in his gut, I think the safest bet is for me to clear the intestines. It's going to mean a stomach tube, unfortunately, so you'll need to keep him still for me."

"OK," Marion said. "Amy and I will hold him."

Amy took firm hold of Sundance's halter. "But he isn't supposed to stand still for long. What happens if he tries to roll?"

Scott looked sombre. "We'll just have to hope we can keep him on his feet. He isn't going to get better without this treatment."

Amy nodded and pulled Sundance's head close. "Listen to me, Sunny. You've got to stand still for us, OK? Just be a good boy and you'll be all right, I promise."

She kept on murmuring the promise over and over to Sundance as Scott manoeuvred the long, slim tube down the gelding's throat to administer the draught of mineral oil. Sundance stumbled back in response to the feel of the pipe, and Amy braced herself against his weight. She pressed her cheek close to Sundance's golden neck as she felt him quiver. Her heart shuddered at the thought that she was the cause of this dreadful night.

Sundance's nostrils flared as Scott raised the bottle of

mineral oil and poured it into the mouth of the tube. Amy tried to shut out the noise as the oil gurgled down the tube, and concentrated instead on whispering comforting words into Sundance's tawny ear.

"OK," Scott said at last, drawing out the endless length of tube from Sundance's throat. "That's all I can do for him now, except to give him some morphine to kill the pain."

Marion began to tell Scott the remedies that she'd already given Sundance. Amy let the rope hang slackly in her hands as she waited to hear Scott's response. Suddenly the pony stiffened. He began pawing at the ground and lowered his head as if he was about to roll. "Get him moving!" Scott shouted at the same time as Marion grabbed the halter.

"Come on!" Amy's fingers gripped the rope, and she heaved against him, determined to keep him on his feet. "Let's go!" she cried as she felt the rope go slack and Sundance gave up fighting her. She walked him on alone, leaving her mom with Scott and Grandpa.

Amy lost count of the circles she paced, hearing just snatches of the conversation between Marion, Jack and Scott. She heard ominous words drift from their conversation, and concentrated instead on putting one foot in front of the other, keeping Sundance plodding beside her. If he didn't work through this, if the sand caused a blockage in his intestine and it eventually twisted, they might have to consider surgery. And even that wasn't a guarantee that he would recover.

Amy was still pacing the yard when the vet was driving away, the taillights of his Jeep disappearing to leave only the sound of Sundance clopping slowly over the surface of the yard.

"What did Scott say?" Amy called.

Marion shot her a quick, tense look. "That there's no way of knowing which way Sundance will go. We've done everything we can, but if Sundance gets worse, then we should give him a call. He said it's all right to let him rest in between spasms so he doesn't get too exhausted."

"OK," Amy said, taking in her mom's words. But she saw Marion's face crease with concern at the exact moment the lead rein went taut. Amy whipped around to see Sundance's back legs folding underneath him, his haunches collapsing.

"Pull him forward!" Marion shouted, racing over to seize a handful of mane and heave with all her strength. With a groan, Sundance regained his balance. Amy stood beside him, shaking with exertion and fear.

Jack grabbed the lead line from Amy and yanked the pony forward. After taking him a few laps, he walked over to where the funnel lay on the ground. He lifted the funnel and paraffin in his huge, work-roughened hands. "Let's see if this helps with the spasms. Hold his head up and keep it there," he said, sliding the tube into the corner of Sundance's mouth. Amy rushed over and propped the pony's head up. Sundance blinked, showing the whites of his eyes, but let Jack get the tube in place. Marion stood on one side of Sundance and Amy stood on the other. Amy slipped one arm under Sundance's head and wrapped the other around his neck, her fingers tangled in his thick mane.

Sundance groaned and shuddered as Jack tipped the fluid into the funnel.

"You're so brave. You really are, Sundance," Amy told him, her cheek pressed against his hot, damp one. Her throat constricted at the sharp, medicinal smell of the drench mingled with Sundance's sweat.

When all of the liquid had drained down the tube, the gelding leaned heavily against Amy, resting his head on her shoulder. She felt a fierce burst of love shoot through her, and a fresh wave of determination that she'd fight for this pony, whatever it took. All her contempt faded, and she found a new commitment as she walked the pony around the moonlit yard.

Her mom and Jack looked exhausted. "There's nothing more to do. It's up to him now," Marion said, pushing her fringe under her barn hat. She pulled back her hair, which hung damply on her shoulders, and Amy realized that the drench must have spilled on her.

"I'll stay with him. You guys look worn out. Go inside and I'll yell if I need you, I promise," Amy told them.

Marion and Jack exchanged reluctant glances. "I'll be OK," Amy insisted. "There's no point in all of us being exhausted tomorrow – there'll still be barn chores to do. Besides, if Sundance needs attention in the morning, someone will have to take over for me." She dropped her voice and ran her hand down Sundance's nose.

Marion bit her lip.

"It's OK. He's my responsibility. I ... I just didn't see that before."

"OK," Marion said at last. "I understand. But if you need us, you yell. Promise?"

Amy nodded, and seeing Sundance's eyes stretch wide, the all-too-familiar sign of an oncoming spasm, she quickly walked him forward. The pony tripped after her, too exhausted by pain to offer any resistance. By the time she had completed a circle of the yard, her mother and grandpa were inside the house.

"It's just the two of us now, boy," she whispered. She slid her hand under Sundance's neck and moved her fingers in slow circles just as her mom had done. Sundance looked at her, his eyes huge with pain. He seemed to be pleading with her to help.

"Oh, Sundance," Amy murmured. She thought back to the time when she had first seen the buckskin gelding at the auction, all teeth and threats. She realized he'd been fighting all of his life, and she wondered what had happened in his past to make him so defensive. But tonight, Amy knew those defences were down. He was willing to let someone help him, and Amy was committed to being the one he could rely on. *If you pull through, I will never let you down again,* she promised silently. She now knew why Sundance had never bonded with her; she had been just another person who had disappointed him. She felt her eyes fill with tears as she wrapped her arm over the pony's neck. "If you come through this – and you'd better – I will always be there for you," she told him.

Sundance sighed heavily and let out a small moan. Amy immediately began walking him again. She talked to keep herself awake, but also to let Sundance know she was still there, that she was still with him. She told him that his getting better was all that mattered. Shows, ribbons, and proving Ashley Grant wrong weren't important – she just wanted to be able to take him on the trails again and feel him buck for the sheer joy of being alive.

Hours passed, with the yard lit by the moon and the softer, yellow light spilling from the kitchen window. Each time Amy rested Sundance for a few moments, he leaned his head on her shoulder and breathed warmly into her hair. Amy's whole world focused on the buckskin pony.

Just before dawn, she halted Sundance and decided to massage more oil into his flanks. Her head was thick with fatigue. She pulled back the cooler and began rubbing the oil on to his coat in deep, rhythmic circles. Sundance stayed still for a longer time than he had all night, and Amy felt a spark of hope that the pain was finally waning. *Please, oh please, let him be getting better,* she thought as she watched Sundance close his eyes. But then they flared open again and he snorted in fright, his body tightening as a spasm ripped through his abdomen. Amy dropped the oil and reached for the lead rope just as Sundance whipped his head around and bit at his stomach. Amy ducked away and grabbed the lead rope with trembling hands.

"Walk on," she urged.

She had been wrong to think the colic had eased. Reluctantly, Sundance lifted a foot to follow her, but then let out a long, low groan unlike anything Amy had ever heard. Spinning around, she saw Sundance's legs buckling beneath him. "No!" she cried.

Sundance's front knees were already crushed against the concrete, and Amy knew she had only seconds to try and pull him back up again before he was fully down and rolling.

"No, Sundance, no!" she yelled. She bent down and reached around his neck, grasping desperately at his mane. She could feel the heat rising from him as she pulled with everything that was inside her. "Please, Sunny. You've got to fight. You can do it," she sobbed. Amy heaved against the weight of the pony, but he only dropped his hindquarters closer to the ground. Then Amy let go of his neck, grabbed his halter, and looked Sundance in the eye.

"I dare you," she said. "I dare you to get up and fight this." She was heartbroken when Sundance continued to pull against her. She pulled harder. And then he grunted and shifted under his own weight, his hooves scraping against the concrete. With a snort, he scrambled back to his feet. He was trembling with exhaustion, but Amy reached back to check his stomach. His flanks were smooth again. The spasm had passed.

Amy wrapped her arms around his neck and kissed him. "I'll never let you go," she whispered into his damp coat. "And you'll never get rid of me. Never."

Sundance turned his head and lipped at her hair. "Come on," Amy said, taking hold of his lead rope again. "We've got some walking to do."

By the time the first grey fingers of dawn spread over the horizon, she was leaning against Sundance, her eyes flickering closed. When she felt a nudge in her side, she sprang upright — her first thought was that Sundance was about to go down again. She looked straight into the gelding's eyes as he nudged her again, and she felt an inkling of hope. Amy slipped her hand under his blanket and felt his stomach. The tightness and swelling had disappeared, and Amy giddily pushed at his belly, relieved that it felt healthy again.

"You're OK!" She hugged the pony's head to her chest. "You're going to be OK," she declared, tears spilling down her cheeks. Sundance playfully nodded his head, and Amy remembered that it was Christmas Day.

Chapter Eleven

The kitchen door opened and Marion appeared, bleary-eyed. She stared at Amy and raised her eyebrows.

"He's OK!" Amy called, her voice choked with emotion.

Marion ran to them and quickly took in the gelding's pricked ears, clear eyes, and relaxed posture. "Do you know, I think you're right!" A smile lit up her face. "Merry Christmas, sweetheart!" She came over and held out her arms. Amy flung herself into them and Marion hugged her tight. "I'm so proud of you. You were there for Sundance when he really needed you. You really helped him get through it, Amy. He wouldn't have made it without you." She squeezed her again and then went to rub Sundance's nose. "Good boy," she told him.

Marion's eyes widened when Sundance pulled away from her to push his nose against Amy's chest. Amy reached up to massage the base of the pony's small golden ears.

"I feel so bad, knowing that it was my fault," she said quietly, biting her lip. "It's not just that he got colic, but I let him down in other ways, too. I feel like I want to earn back his trust, no matter what. I know he'll be rehomed soon, but I'll do whatever I can so he believes in me before he goes…" Her voice trailed off as she faced the fact that she had made Sundance promises that she wouldn't be able to keep. She meant it when she had said she'd never let him go, but she knew she had to. It was the way Heartland worked – once the horses were healthy and adjusted, Marion would seek out a new owner who would provide a loving home. Amy knew the rules, but she had never felt like this before. Just when she had made her true bond with Sundance, she had to let him go.

"I think he's forgiven me," she said in an excited whisper.

"I tend to believe that horses are the most forgiving creatures in the world," Marion said gently. "After what the two of you have been through, I think you are both ready to wipe the slate clean and start anew."

Amy nodded.

"I think we can take him inside now," her mom went on, patting Sundance's neck. "He should be fine."

"I'll fix him a nice, deep bed," Amy decided.

"Sounds good," said Marion. "I, however, will require a cup of coffee before I start the morning feeds."

Amy clicked to Sundance and began to lead him towards the barn, then hesitated. She knew there was a lot more involved in helping Sundance recover than walking laps around the yard. "Mom?" she called over her shoulder.

Marion was pulling open the kitchen door. "Yes?"

"I was wondering, would you teach me some more about your remedies?" Amy asked carefully. "I'd like to know more about them, if that's OK."

Her mom's face lit up. "That would be more than OK," she said warmly. "It's something I've always wanted to do, but I didn't know if you'd be interested. Oh, I'm so excited, Amy. That's the best Christmas present you could have given me."

Amy watched her mom bound up the slight hill to the house, and she wondered what she had got herself into. Her mom would no doubt have her immersed in the canon of holistic horse remedies by nightfall. Still, Amy wasn't too put off by the prospect. She clicked to Sundance and led the tired horse back to his stall.

As she was adding yet another layer of straw to Sundance's bed, she heard the rest of the barn come to life with whinnies, clanging buckets, and contented chewing.

"Merry Christmas, dear!" Jack leaned over the door with the proud smile of a grandfather. "Would the heroine of the night like some celebratory muffins?"

Amy laughed. She suddenly realized that she hadn't eaten since her trip to the mall with Soraya. "Are you kidding? I could eat the whole batch."

"Oh, but that wouldn't be in the holiday spirit," Marion advised as she walked up to the stall. "Scott's on his way to check on Sundance. He's a real trooper to come on Christmas." She looked Amy up and down, taking in her tearstained cheeks and the countless strands of light brown hair escaping from her ponytail. "Speaking of troopers, I think you should take a shower now and try to get some sleep."

"I want to stay with Sundance," Amy said stubbornly.

She expected her mother to argue, but instead Marion playfully shook her head. "Hey, who does she remind you of?" she asked Jack.

"Oh, yes. I see it. The resemblance is uncanny," he said, stroking his chin.

Amy frowned. "Who?"

"Me!" Marion laughed. "I can't tell you how many times I've curled up in Pegasus's stall when he was sick."

Amy's eyes gleamed. "Now, there's an idea."

Marion reached over to squeeze her hand. Amy knew by her expression that she understood exactly how devoted her daughter was to Sundance.

Amy crammed the last piece of muffin into her mouth and licked at a stray drop of blueberry filling that was dribbling down her chin. "That was delicious," she said. "Thanks, Grandpa."

Jack had found an old Christmas record in his room and brought it down with his ancient record player, which he refused to part with. He had set it up in the corner of the kitchen for them to listen to the charming crackle of carols and songs while they ate a late breakfast. Marion had tied her hair back with red tinsel and was singing loudly as she cleared the plates. Amy couldn't remember a better Christmas morning ever. So what if the tree wasn't trimmed, they didn't have a turkey, and the cards weren't hanging up? Sundance was better, and that was the most amazing Christmas present she could have.

Amy heard a car in the drive and looked out the window. It was Scott's Jeep. Amy grabbed her coat and pulled it on as she opened the door. When she reached the stable, Scott was just putting his stethoscope back in his bag. "Well," he smiled, "it looks like Sundance is this year's Christmas miracle, thanks to you and your mom. He should be fine, but don't give him any hard feed today. He can have a small amount of hay and water, but that's it."

"OK." Amy nodded, smoothing Sundance's neck. "I'm going to stay with him all day, so I'll make sure that he takes it easy."

"Well, I don't think that's necessary. In fact, Sundance might appreciate it if you took a shower," Scott offered, laughing to himself. He held up one hand as Amy lifted her chin mutinously.

"OK, OK. You can do what you want. But, Amy – you should know that you did a good job last night. He's lucky to have had you taking care of him."

Amy thought about what Scott had said as they walked up to the house. She was so relieved that Sundance had recovered, but part of her regretted the promises she had made to him. She didn't want to be just another person who deserted him. She wanted to prove that she deserved his trust.

When they reached the drive, Scott got in his Jeep and Amy headed inside. The kitchen was disturbingly empty, but Amy thought she heard muffled sounds from the living room.

"Surprise!"

Marion and Jack were comically posed around the Christmas tree, which was all aglow with twinkle lights and three shades of tinsel. Lou's icicles hung from the tips of the branches, and the Swedish wooden decorations were nestled further inside. Marion was standing on a ladder, putting a homemade angel on top of the tree. Amy recognized it as one that Lou had made in school years and years ago, and while its cone-shaped base was a little dented, it still shone with gold glitter.

"Perfect!" Marion declared as she secured the angel.

"Oh, wow! I'd given up all hope that we'd have decorations!" Amy exclaimed. "After last night, it just didn't seem that important."

"Well, in that case..." Jack teased, pretending to unhook one of the icicles.

"Don't you dare!" Amy said. "It's beautiful."

After giving the tree a thorough investigation, Amy flew upstairs for a quick shower and pulled on a clean pair of jeans and a thick sweater before heading back down to the stable. Her mom was already there, letting herself out of Jasmine's stall. "The swelling's definitely going down in her legs," she declared. "I should think we'll be able to walk her around the paddock tomorrow."

Amy felt as if her spirits couldn't get any higher.

At the sound of her footsteps, Sundance let out a low, welcoming nicker. He was lying down on the thick bed of straw, looking tired but relaxed, his ears pricked forward as he watched Amy's every movement.

"Here." Marion handed Amy a plastic bottle with a spray handle. "It's a spritzer made from caraway, peppermint, fennel, jupiter, lavender —" she raised her eyes upward for a moment to think — "and coriander and cumin," she finished. "Spray it around the stall. The scent will help him relax, which will hopefully ease any remaining stomachache."

"I'll never remember everything that you know," Amy

sighed, taking the bottle and spraying it in a fine cloud in the corners of the stall. The mist smelled sweet, with a tangy hint of spice.

"Yes, you will," Marion said reassuringly. "We'll go through everything a little bit at a time. Don't forget, I've been doing this for more than ten years now, and I'm still learning. Now –" she sounded brisk again – "I'd better get these horses turned out before it's time to bring them back in."

"What's all this slacking off? What do you think it is, a holiday?" a familiar voice teased. Amy peeped over the stall door and smiled at Ty, who was walking up the aisle towards them.

"Don't ask!" Marion said. "We've had quite a night."

"Why don't I give you a hand putting the horses out and you can tell me about it?" Ty offered.

"Hang on a minute. You aren't supposed to be here at all! I can't have you working on Christmas Day. It's against union policy," Marion protested, but Ty was already fetching an armful of halters from the tack room.

Amy turned her attention back to Sundance. Her heart felt full as she knelt down beside him in the straw and began to move her hand in small circles on his neck. One of the first things she wanted her mom to show her was how to do T-touch properly. "I'm so proud of you," she murmured, watching his ear flick back at the sound of her voice. She didn't know how she was going to face the moment when he ended up going to a new home. *I wish you could stay here with me,* she thought, feeling an intense sadness stealing over her as she realized that this time next year Sundance would be in a different stall, with different people taking care of him.

She tried to push the thought away and concentrate instead on everything wonderful that had happened over the last twelve hours. Sundance had pulled through in spite of everything, and for the first time ever, Amy felt like she might be able to make a real contribution to her mom's unique healing work at Heartland. It wasn't just about riding the horses – although she knew she'd never stop enjoying that – it was about caring for them with all the knowledge and dedication that her mom had built up over the years. Amy smiled as she pictured all the seasons ahead that she would share with her mom on the yard – crisp winters and warm summers – to the constant echo of hoofbeats.

She listened to the rhythmic sound of Sundance's breathing against the louder noise of horses' hooves clattering down the aisle, and found her eyes closing. She must have dozed off for a while, because the next thing she knew, Ty was kneeling down in the straw beside her. Amy felt flushed after just waking up, and she pushed the hair out of her face.

"Hey, your mom told me what happened," he said, his green eyes serious. "It sounds like you were great."

Amy looked down and fiddled with Sundance's mane. "I can't take the credit. It was all Sundance. He knew he had to fight, and that's what he did," she said.

Ty shook his head. "I'm all for giving the pony credit, but he couldn't have done it without you. It took a lot of courage and love – on both your parts. I knew you two would work things out." He pulled out a small package from his inside coat pocket. "Here," he said. "Merry Christmas."

"But your gift is in the house," Amy told him. "Will you get it before you go?" Ty nodded, watching her reaction as she unwrapped the present.

Amy took in a deep breath as she turned over the silver picture frame and looked at the photograph inside. It had been taken in the summer at the last show she had ridden Sundance in. Amy was accepting an impressive silver cup, and there was a blue ribbon pinned to Sundance's bridle.

"I didn't know you'd taken this!" she exclaimed. "It's one of the nicest gifts anyone's ever given me. Thank you, Ty."

Ty smiled as he stood up, his feet rustling in the straw. "You should try to get some more sleep," he said. "I'm sorry I woke you."

"That's OK. I'm glad you did," Amy said, lying back down and resting her head near Sundance's. The gelding shifted slightly and sighed. Amy closed her eyes, and almost immediately slipped into blissful clouds of sleep once again.

"Hey, sleepyhead." Her mom's voice woke Amy this time. She felt groggy and disoriented, and it took her a few moments to figure out where she was.

"You've been asleep for four hours," Marion told her. "Lunch is ready, so come in now. Sundance will be fine on his own for a while. If you stay out here much longer, Santa might bring you hooves and a tail!"

Amy looked down at the gelding stretched out on the straw.

She patted him gently and stood up, smiling as Sundance scrambled to his feet, too, shaking himself thoroughly with a drawn-out groan.

"I think the rest has done you both good," said Marion, holding the door open for her.

"I do feel better," Amy admitted.

"Soraya called earlier," Marion added. "I brought her up to date and promised that you'd call her back later."

Jack was on the phone when they walked into the kitchen. He beckoned to them both. "It's Lou, she wants to talk to you," he said.

Amy took the phone. "Merry Christmas," she said, hearing the background noise of a party on her sister's end of the line. She couldn't feel angry with Lou any more for leaving early. It was just good to talk to her and know that she was thinking of them.

"And to you," said Lou, her voice raised over the noise. "Are you having a good day?"

"The best," Amy said, smiling at her mom and grandpa. "Except, I guess it would be better if you were here."

"Oh, I'm missing you all so much. It's weird, now that I'm back, I'm feeling nostalgic for Heartland. The holidays just aren't the same without family." To Amy's surprise, there was a wistful note in Lou's voice.

"We miss you, too," Amy told her. "If you promise not to wait so long to come back again, I'll promise not to spend your whole visit in the barn."

"That's a deal," Lou agreed. "Besides, we might meet up

sooner than you think. I already ran it past Mom, and she said it's OK. I've bought tickets for a show, and I want you to come and spend the weekend with me next month. It's my Christmas present for you. I want to be able to spend some real time with you," Lou said. "We can do some shopping and then order pizza and watch movies. I promise it will be low-key – just the two of us."

"That would be great," Amy replied, thinking that Lou's plans didn't sound too big-city, just like a lot of sisterly fun.

Amy passed the phone to Marion and flipped through the book on show jumping that Matt had given her until they were ready for dinner. It might not have been the traditional turkey, but it still tasted delicious – and Grandpa had even found a jar of ready-made cranberry sauce left over from Thanksgiving. Amy thought she couldn't have asked for more until Marion handed her a card.

"What's this?"

"An extra present for you, because of everything you did last night," Marion told her, exchanging a telling look with Jack.

"Aren't we going to open all of the gifts after lunch?" Amy asked.

"Well, this one is kind of special." Marion explained.

Amy slipped her thumb under the flap and opened the envelope. It wasn't a card at all. There was only a thin, folded piece of paper inside. She pulled it out and unfolded it, narrowing her eyes as she tried to decipher the mixture of legal print and faded writing.

"An old receipt?" she said, feeling puzzled. And then recognition slowly dawned on her. She looked up. "It's the bill of sale for Sundance." Her voice trembled, not daring to hope what it meant. "It's what we got from the auction house when we first bought him."

Marion nodded, tears forcing their way out of her eyes as she smiled. "He's yours," she said softly. "After last night, you deserve to be with each other. I know we could never find an owner who would love him more."

Amy felt her own eyes overflow with tears as she stared from her mother to her grandpa. She blinked them back furiously.

"I don't know, Marion. She doesn't look so happy to me. Maybe we should have given her something else. I don't like to see the poor girl in tears," said Jack, shaking his head slowly.

"Are you kidding?" Amy pushed back her chair and flung her arms around her mom and then her grandpa. "It's the best present you could ever have given me. Thank you, thank you! I won't let you down." Leaving them both breathless and laughing, she tore outside without even stopping to pull on her coat.

Her feet pounded down the aisle, echoing around the barn. Sundance nickered when she pulled open the stall door, and leaving it open, Amy threw her arms around his neck.

"You're mine," she said, her voice choked with emotion. "Do you hear that, boy? Heartland is your home now — for ever!"

Chapter Twelve

It was the day before Amy went back to school, and her alarm woke her early. She blinked a few times, wondering why her stomach felt full of butterflies, until she remembered what was planned for that morning. Scott was coming to give Sundance a final check-up, and as long as he was fully recovered, Marion was going to take Amy through her first-ever join-up.

She pulled back the curtains and saw early morning sunlight creeping over the stable block, reflecting brightly off the whitewashed doors. Marion was leading Pegasus down to the top field while Ty was walking across the yard, muffled in a wool scarf and swinging a halter in his hand. Amy felt another surge of nerves mixed with excitement and let the curtain drop. She grabbed her jeans and a sweater from the chair and pulled them on.

"Morning, sweetheart!" Jack called as she hurried through the kitchen. "Do you want some pancakes?"

"Maybe later. Thanks, Grandpa," she said, taking her coat off the hook and pushing her arms through the sleeves.

Amy headed straight for the feed room and mixed a measure of cod liver oil with Sundance's morning feed. She had taken over his entire care since Christmas Day and was still basking in the thrill of their new, improved relationship. While they hadn't entered the holiday show because of his illness, Amy knew they didn't need a ribbon to prove the strength of their bond.

"Morning, boy," she called, smiling at the sight of Sundance's golden head looking for her over the door. He gave a long, high whinny, which was still echoing around the barn when she set the bucket down in his stall. Whistling, Amy patted his shoulder before going to collect the wheelbarrow and fork to muck out his stall. She had been taken by surprise at how much she enjoyed caring for Sundance, when she had been so focused on the riding before. Now, she felt she had even more in common with her mom, who was teaching her a new herb and its uses every day. There seemed to be so many, Amy imagined it would take her about twenty years to learn everything her mom knew!

After his breakfast, Sundance came back to the door, ignoring his hay net. He kicked at the back of his stall, making it rattle loudly.

"Easy, boy," Amy told him. She was just leading Jasmine down the aisle. The black mare was now allowed an hour each day in the paddock with the other horses. She was proving to be every inch the sweet pony that Amy and Marion had suspected she was, and she had become a real favourite with everyone, especially Soraya. Amy's best friend had been beside herself with excitement when Marion suggested that she might like to help out with the mare's reschooling.

Sundance bared his teeth and snapped at Jasmine, who was fortunately out of reach. "Sundance!" Amy scolded. Over the last few days, the buckskin's uncertain temper had returned along with his strength. The one difference was that where Amy had previously been privy to the worst of his moods, she was now the one person whom he not only tolerated, but seemed to adore.

"I'll come back for you in a minute," Amy promised, leading Jasmine down the aisle and out into the sunshine. When she turned her into the top paddock, the black mare let out a contented sigh and ambled away to graze alongside Casper and Jupiter.

Amy went back to the barn to help finish the mucking out before returning to Sundance. He had given up waiting for her and was snatching at his hay net. "Stop sulking," she told him, unbuckling his stable blanket and beginning to groom him with long, smooth strokes.

When she had finished, she clipped on his lead rope and led him out on to the yard. Scott was there already, chatting with Marion. He smiled when he saw them. "That's a very different pony from the one I saw on Christmas Day," he remarked. "Trot him down to the top of the path and back again. Let's see how he does."

Amy nodded. She had been taking Sundance for gentle walks by hand since he had been ill, and she was hopeful that Scott would pronounce him well enough for more strenuous exercise now. She trotted him up and down while Scott watched Sundance carefully. Amy couldn't help but feel a rush of pride in the way the gelding arched his neck and lifted his knees high with each step.

Next, Scott listened to Sundance's breathing, pressing his

stethoscope along his flanks before straightening up. "He's fine," he pronounced.

"Did you hear that?" Amy beamed as she patted Sundance's shoulder.

"Take it easy for the next week," Scott warned. "No jumping, just work him on the flat." He put his bag back into his Jeep before climbing in and pulling the door shut. "See you soon," he called.

"Hopefully not too soon," Amy joked.

Marion joined her, carrying a coiled-up lunge line. She walked with an extra-long stride, the ends of her wavy blonde hair peeping out from under her bright red wool hat. "Ready?" she asked.

Amy's stomach turned over. "Ready," she answered.

They walked down to the arena in silence, and by the time they were standing in the middle of the ring, Amy had convinced herself that she would make a mess of the whole thing. The process of joining up was completely different from riding a horse, because it was based on fear.

"What happens if Sundance thinks I'm rejecting him when I drive him away? I don't want him to turn against me. I don't want to be back to square one," she said with a note of panic in her voice.

Marion put her hands on Amy's shoulders and looked deep into her eyes. "Do you trust me?"

Amy nodded, biting her lower lip.

"Then you have to believe me when I say this will make your bond with Sundance even stronger. It will strengthen his faith in you, so that when you ride him again, he will see you as his partner. You'll be a team." Marion's eyes met Amy's, solemn and searching.

Amy felt stirred by her mother's promise. She took a deep, shaky breath. "I'm ready."

"Good girl," Marion said, reaching out to unsnap Sundance's lead rope. "Now, I'm going to stay by you and talk you through what you need to do."

"OK," Amy nodded.

"Here," Marion said, handing her the lunge line. "Flick this at his hindquarters to send him out to the fence."

Amy took the lunge rein in her hand. She didn't know how she could bring herself to chase Sundance away. Marion placed her hand over Amy's and moved it so that the end of the rein flicked against Sundance's quarters.

Sundance snorted in surprise and moved sideways.

"Again," Marion urged, taking her hand off Amy's. Amy tightened her hold on the rein and flicked it again. This time Sundance broke into a trot, moving close to the fence. Amy flicked the rein one last time to send him into a canter. "Good," Marion said behind her. "You've got the hang of it!"

"Don't leave me!" Amy panicked.

"It's OK, I'm staying right here. Now, step forward," her mom directed.

Licking her dry lips, Amy took a step in line with Sundance's head, and her heart skipped as he slowed down. Without her mom prompting her, she took a step back and watched with delight as Sundance quickened his pace. He was giving Amy textbook responses, reacting as if she were chasing him. Even though it felt strange to be driving Sundance away, Amy was thrilled at how closely he was watching her, reacting to her slightest movement.

"Good," her mom said again.

Amy barely heard her. All of her attention was focused on Sundance. The buckskin's inside ear was turned towards her as he cantered around the ring, his tail streaming behind him in the brisk wind.

Around and around he went until Amy's heart quickened. Sundance had started lowering his head to the ground, his nostrils flaring.

"He's showing you that he doesn't want to run away from you any more," Marion said softly.

Amy kept him moving, hardly daring to believe the signs that she was seeing. But when Sundance began to open and close his mouth she knew for sure that the join-up was working.

"Now," Marion said, "turn your back to him. This lets him know that he has no reason to be afraid of you, because you aren't trying to chase him any more."

Slowly, Amy turned away from the cantering pony. Nothing happened for several anxious moments, and she began to think it hadn't worked and that she'd alienated him for ever. She started to turn around, and then heard the sweetest of sounds – Sundance's hooves thudding over the sand towards her. Amy dug her nails into her palms when she heard him snort just behind her. He padded to a halt and nudged her gently with his nose. All she wanted to do was turn and throw her arms around him, but she knew she couldn't. Join-up involved an additional, telling step.

"What are you waiting for?" Her mom's voice was warm. "Walk away from him."

With her heart racing, Amy took three steps forward and waited until Sundance joined her again. Step by step, she walked across the arena, aware that for every stride she took, Sundance followed. Marion led the way, walking backward with her gaze fixed on Amy.

When she stopped just feet away from her mother, Amy could see that her mom's eyes were bright with joy. She shook her head slowly. "You were incredible," Marion said. "It takes a lot of courage to send a horse away, but Sundance chose to come back to you – I knew he would."

A look of respect and understanding passed between them, and then Amy turned and threw her arms around Sundance. "We did it," she whispered. She held out a mint for Sundance and pressed her cheek against his. She knew that however many join-ups she did in the future with other horses that needed her help, nothing would ever come close to this moment. *This is what I was meant to do,* she thought, stroking Sundance's nose. *I know where I belong.*

Epilogue

Lou sighed and tried to straighten out the wing on the angel that was dented from having been stored away for another year. "I still can't believe that I went back to New York to spend Christmas with Carl. What was I thinking?"

"That's what *I* want to know!" Amy agreed. "He was such a jerk."

Lou shook her head playfully. "It's OK, don't feel like you have to choose your words carefully. Feel free to say just what you think of my ex-boyfriend!"

"You know what I mean," Amy said, smiling.

Then Lou's expression turned serious. She added in a low voice, "I know Mom tried to put on a brave face when I left like that, but I bet she was really disappointed. I feel like I let her down."

"She *was* disappointed," Amy admitted, feeling a brief pang as she recalled that Lou hadn't been the only one to disappoint their mom that Christmas. "But at the same time, she understood. Mom said how proud she was of you and your independence. I think she really admired you for going to New York and making it there."

Lou looked thoughtful. "I don't know. To tell you the truth, it seemed a lot easier than being here. Not better, just easier," she explained.

Amy knew how much time and effort Lou put in now to keep Heartland successful – how much she had brought to their mother's life's work. "And considering you didn't ride then," Amy went on. "Mom also said that she felt bad that we had been so focused on the horses, and that we hadn't really gone out of our way to include you."

"Well, I won't pretend that I didn't feel a little left out, but I didn't try all that hard, either. And it didn't help that I let a lame pony loose, remember? I can see why you were annoyed with me."

"What's with the past tense?" Amy teased, ducking to avoid her sister's swat.

"I'm glad you told me that Mom felt that way. I know she always wanted us to be true to ourselves, whether that was in New York, or Heartland, or wherever," Lou said quietly. "I never thought back then that I would ever see Heartland as my home. But now I can't imagine being anywhere else."

Amy nodded and got to her feet, rubbing her legs where they were aching. "You belong here, even though it took a while for us all to realize it!" She smiled, thinking of all the battles she and Lou had fought when her sister first moved in. "Mom would be so proud to know that we're carrying on her work together."

"Oh, I'm sure she does know," Lou said softly, her eyes bright.

Amy crouched down again to pick up the box of decorations. "We'd better get going. They'll be sending out a search party if we don't head back downstairs. Besides, I want some cookies before they're all gone."

"Well, just so you know," Lou said conspiratorially, leading the way and holding the door open, "I put a secret stash in the pantry. They're in the green tin."

As Amy stepped into the hallway, she thought that things between her and Lou felt lighthearted once again. But Amy was glad that she and Lou had been able to talk so honestly about the last Christmas with their mother. That was one of the nice things about having a sister, Amy reflected. Having someone to share a memory with brought new life and meaning to the past.

As she made her way carefully down the stairs, Amy thought about Lou's words. She was right: Marion had always wanted her daughters to follow their hearts, even if that took them away from Heartland. But Amy would never forget the look of joy in her mom's eyes the day she had joined up with Sundance. Marion's legacy was a wonderful one, and Amy knew that she carried a part of her mother inside her, which would only strengthen with each horse she healed.

"Finally!" Scott greeted them, taking the box from Amy.

"We were beginning to think we'd have to celebrate Christmas without you!" Ty added, his green eyes twinkling.

Jack picked up the angel. "My favourite decorations are the homemade ones," he smiled. "Your mom told me that the day you made this, Lou, you came home from school with more glitter in your hair than on the angel."

They all laughed, and Scott and Ty reached into the box at the same time to draw out the wooden decorations. "My mom and dad bought those in Sweden when they were on the World Cup tour," Amy explained as she claimed the round box of Manhattan icicles and looked for long, strong branches for the elegant ornaments.

Lou picked up the stepladder that was leaning against the sofa and placed it next to the tree. She climbed up and reached her hand out to Amy for the angel. Lou carefully placed it on the top of the tree and then climbed down, stepping back to check that it was straight.

For a moment, Amy thought her sister looked just like Marion, admiring the battered angel on their last Christmas together. This moment, more than anything else, gave Amy the feeling of a true family Christmas. Whatever happened, Marion would always be with them, in their memories and in their hearts.

"What do you think?" Lou asked the group.

"The angel's wings are kind of crooked," Scott said, tipping his head to one side as he looked at the decoration.

"I can fix her." Jack put his foot on the first step of the ladder.

"No!" Lou and Amy spoke together.

Amy smiled as Ty, Scott and Grandpa looked equally baffled.

"Let's not change anything about her," Amy said, thinking of how much her mom had loved the angel. "She looks perfect just the way she is."

There's always
something going on in

ALLY'S WORLD

Make sure you keep up with the gossip!

1 ## the PAST, the PRESENT and the LOUD, LOUD GIRL

My family's weird – I know everyone says that, but trust me – we are definitely weird. My eldest sister is 17 going on 70, my other sister is away with the fairies (literally – her room is a shrine to whoever invented fairy lights) and my little brother is a space cadet who's obsessed with Rolf Harris. Me? Somehow I ended up normal, but it's a struggle, let me tell you – and I will tell you – soon as I get this vibrating three-legged cat off my head...

2 DATES, DOUBLE DATES and BIG, BIG TROUBLE

OK, so my dad's started ironing his jeans (yes, really) – something must be up. I mean, why would he slick back his hair to meet the plumber? It can only mean one thing – Dad is Seeing Someone. Like, a Woman Someone. And it can't be our mum, because she's still off travelling the world. There's only one thing for it – serious sisterly espionage. Hey, I know it's sneaky, but we have to uncover the awful (cringe-worthy) truth...

3 BUTTERFLIES, BULLIES and BAD, BAD HABITS

Rowan's been acting strange (well, OK, more strange than usual). One minute she's crying over who-knows-what, and the next she's tripping into the house with all this new stuff (which has to come from the shopping fairy, since I know she's got zero money). Then there's the graffiti at school: "Rowan Love is a muppet" (and I don't think it's meant in a friendly, Kermit-is-cool kind of way). Just what is going on with my sister?

4 FRiENDs, FREAK-OUTS and VERY SECRET SECRETS

OK, so I did have a best friend called Sandie, but I think she's been replaced by a Star-Trek type android. She still looks like Sandie, but since when did my real friend copy everything I do, and storm off in big huffs over nothing? I think the same thing's happened to Kyra's mum – the super-witch mum from hell Kyra's always moaning about actually seems super-nice. Have all my mates gone mad, or have I stumbled into Crouch End in a parallel universe...?!

5 BOYS, bROTHERS and JELLY-BELLY dANCiNG

Boys are weird things ... and just lately, the boys in my life have been acting even more weird. Take Billy, for example. He's been behaving like a total muppet (as the whole bra-on-head incident proves), and what's worse is I've been having unexplained feelings (like – eek! – lovey, jealous type feelings) for the big dweeb (scary). Not only that, but Tor's been acting strange too – something to do with boy mice, girl mice, and Mum. Confused? You're not the only one...

6 SISTERS, SUPER-CREEPS & SLUSHY, GUSHY LOVE SONGS

So Linn isn't usually the most approachable elder sister (about as approachable as a grumpy wasp), but her "My family drives me mad!!" face has definitely been appearing more often lately. Maybe trespassing in her sacred room to answer her mobile wasn't one of my best ideas... Still, now we know that Linn's got a boyfriend – Q, lead singer in Chazza's band. Linn thinks he's super-cool, so why do me and Rowan get the distinct impression that he's actually a super-creep...?

Look out for loads more fab
Ally's World books!
Find out more about Ally's World at

www.karenmccombie.com